consequences...

Consequences

Look out for:

Laurie Depp

consequences...

Runway girl

Hodder
Children's
Books

A division of Hachette Children's Book

1

If it hadn't been for Stevie, I would never have been a model. YOU OWE IT ALL TO ME; that's how he used to sign off his texts to me. Six months ago the texts stopped. I should have been glad; I used to complain about those texts, a lot. Once, during a really complicated shoot for British *Vogue* (the cast included three ballerinas balancing on horses and a small band of acrobats; I spent three hours on a trapeze) he texted me fifteen times: I'M BORED . . . THE DVD IS BROKE . . . YOU OWE IT ALL TO ME, over and over again.

When I finally got down from the swing, I jabbed out a single, furious reply: I'M WORKING! STOP SHOUTING. It didn't occur to me that he might be missing me. Last night on the beach, I would have given anything for one of Stevie's rude, shouty birthday messages.

On my seventeenth birthday, I was being sewn into a white silk couture dress in a freezing car park in Berlin when the assistant stylist handed me my phone: TOO OLD TO BE JAIL BAIT, TOO YOUNG TO BE A WOMAN. HAPPY BIRTHDAY FREAK XXX PS − YOU OWE IT ALL TO ME.

He was right. You don't have to be beautiful to be a

model, but you do have to be seen. Without Stevie, no model scout in the world could have discovered me. Without Stevie I would have spent the last two years sitting in my bedroom watching Reese Witherspoon romcoms, wishing I was shorter, blonder, perkier.

Stevie said cute blonde girls were fine but he couldn't eat a whole one. He didn't so much build my self-esteem up as tear the rest of the world down, until we were the only two people left standing. The pretty girls all the other boys at school drooled over were, according to Stevie, 'Plastic' and 'Obvious'. We were Freaks, which was a good thing. When the agency signed me, Stevie acted like the Freaks had won, for all time: 'You see!' he crowed. 'Obvious doesn't cut it.'

I never pointed out to him that plenty of models are totally obvious; they're the prettiest girls at school only prettier. Some of these girls grow up liking what they see in the mirror so much they have to share it with the world. They walk through agency doors at fourteen and are signed on the spot; their mothers are ex-models, ex-actresses, ex-beauties. I was never one of those girls; my mother was never a beauty.

Growing up, I didn't exactly hate what I saw in the mirror, I just didn't expect anybody else to like it. A good day was a day when nobody stared. When I was fifteen I went through a phase of trying to disguise my height. 'You know, when you walk like that –' head drooped forward, shoulders up round the ears '– it makes you look like a hunchback,' quipped Stevie. 'You're tall. Only short-arse idiots have a problem with that.'

Stevie is only five foot four inches. I'm six foot. He doesn't like to mention height – his or mine. It would have cost him something, using an expression like 'short-arse'. I gave up on the Quasimodo thing. Stevie made me walk tall. He got me out of my bedroom. It's because of Stevie I was in the right place at the right time on my sixteenth birthday.

'It's your birthday. You're sixteen! We are going to the Oxford Circus Topshop.'

When Stevie refers to anything or anybody he truly respects, he always says their full name, with, sometimes, a bit of additional information. He started doing it round about the same time as the first series of *The OC*, so I guess he picked it up from Summer, and her not-at-all-annoying habit of calling the world's cutest geek 'Seth Cohen'.

I didn't take much persuading. It was Saturday, it's not like I had anything else planned and, besides, I liked clothes shopping almost as much as Stevie. I muttered something about having no money and couldn't we just watch a DVD, a bit of token resistance, just to give him the thrill of changing my mind.

'You are not spending your birthday in bloody Nowhere!' hissed Stevie. Nowhere was our name for our home town.

'But I live in Nowhere, Stevie,' I said mildly, 'so do you.'

'Exactly!'

Six hours later I was standing in the vintage section of the

Oxford Circus Topshop with nothing to show for our day of fashion pilgrimage except dehydration (the only brand I truly cared about at that moment was Evian) and a large scratch on my cheek from one of the dozens of zips I'd hauled over my head. There are days when clothes cover you like excited puppies, and days when they droop, depressed, the moment you put them on. This was a day when the clothes were suicidal.

'I'm not buying it, Stevie. Let's go. I've had it.' I shoved an inky-blue beaded dress back on the rail – a dress he had made me try on three times – and marched off. I expected a siren wail of protest to follow me but there was nothing. Sometimes Stevie lets you think he's given in, when, in fact, he's just regrouping. I had my foot on the exit escalator when he grabbed my arm and yanked me back.

He hooked the dress over my head (still on its hanger) and barked: 'Look, Freak, you don't have to show your stringy legs. Wear it over jeans – it will be totally fabulous. You'll look like Mischa Barton. From the neck down, I mean.'

'It's too short for me,' I pleaded, 'it will look like a blouse.'

'Exactly,' said Stevie.

I went back and bought the dress. That's why I was on the escalator, going up to the ground floor, at 6.45 p.m. instead of 6.30 p.m., just as Corinne Taylor, head of new talent at Focus Model Management, was on the parallel downwards escalator.

'Hey! Yes, you, girl in the green jacket. Wait for me. I need to speak to you!' It was mortifying. Being spoken to by strangers was my least favourite thing in the world. It was amazing how often people came up to me to tell me that I was, like, tall. I would have bolted but Stevie (typically), who would never knowingly walk away from a scene, clamped his hand to my arm.

'She's acting like a psycho,' he hissed, delighted. I didn't trust myself to speak. It was my birthday, and my best friend, my only real friend, was forcing me to meet a madwoman.

'What's the worst that can happen?' Stevie whispered in my ear, as Corinne stepped off the escalator, looking flustered (she'd run up the steps) but not at all psycho.

'She probably wants to know where you got your fabulous jacket.' This seemed possible. My jacket – a charity shop find I'd taken apart and remade on my Aunt Pat's old sewing machine – was pretty damn fine. I'd shortened the sleeves to three-quarters length and nipped in the waist to turn a seventies horror into fifties chic. I wondered if the crazy woman was going to try and buy my jacket. It had happened before: two months previously a woman came up to me in a Save the Children shop and bought the halterneck top I was wearing for twenty quid; I'd made it out of an old velvet curtain. I shivered all the way home, topless (in every sense) under my parka.

'Good, you're here. Thought I might have scared you away.' Corinne smiled brightly and I thought: you're pretty, like a model. Long brown hair, light golden tan (she was just back from a four-day shoot in Mauritius, I found out later) and skinny. But not like-a-boy skinny, not like me; she was skinny with breasts. She introduced herself, asked my name, and then got straight to the point.

'I love your look. Have you ever considered becoming a model? You should. Come into the agency for a chat. I really think it will be worth your while. You've got something.'

'I've got a – a what?' I was so mesmerised by Corinne's lips – were they that colour naturally or had she found the best lipstick shade in the history of cosmetics? – that I barely heard what she was saying. Stevie, on the other hand, hadn't missed a thing. He wasn't just listening to Corinne; he was inhaling her.

'She wants to make you a model,' he squealed in my ear, 'she's from a proper agency and everything. Focus! I've heard of them. They discovered Francine Hope at Heathrow Airport!'

Corinne smiled that smile again. 'That's right. That was me actually, I spotted Francine. She's doing very well for us.'

Francine retired from modelling last year, aged twenty-five, to launch her own clothing line and raise kids with her girlfriend, Paulette. But two years ago she was 'The Girl who put the Super back in Supermodel' – an old-fashioned eighties-style beauty, all hair and legs and teeth. She was the ultimate Brazil beach babe. (In fact, she's from Texas. The first time she ever stood on a beach she was modelling Versace swimwear. I worked with her a few times. She's nice.)

All this talk of Francine made Corinne's show of interest in me even more bizarre. I sincerely doubted whether

Francine and I were the same species. Could the woman who had 'spotted' the superest super of them all really be saying that I could be a model? I scowled. Corinne put her hand on my arm and steered me and Stevie (who was still attached to my other arm) away from the escalator to a relatively quiet spot near a display of granny-style handbags.

'Are you OK?' she asked, gently.

'Are you taking the piss?' I snapped. Sometimes when I am nervous or upset I can be quite rude. This was one of those times.

'No, really, I'm completely serious.' She took a business card out of a huge white handbag and pressed it into my hand. 'Come and see me, next week.'

'Oh, she will, she will,' panted Stevie, who seemed to be having difficulty breathing. 'Wednesday afternoon suit you?' he said, inexplicably. 'She can do Wednesday.'

Corinne looked a little taken aback. 'Wednesday's fine.' And she smiled and was gone.

You know when something huge happens it can be hard to face up to it straightaway? The detail you can look at, but not the whole thing, not all at once; it's like you can't stand back far enough to take it all in. That's how it was on the train back to Nowhere. I spent the first ten minutes of the journey arguing with Stevie.

'We're at school on Wednesday, or had you forgotten that? Why Wednesday?'

'Why not Wednesday? It's only double maths and

games; we can skip it. I had to say something. You were acting like she'd just cancelled Christmas, not offered to make you a star. Focus Management are going to make you a model. In real life!'

'Come in for a chat she said, that's all she said, and now you've said I will, and I'll go and she'll realise she's made a mistake and it'll be awful and it'll be all your fault! You're always making me do things I don't want to and I'm sick of it!'

'You mentalist!' shrieked Stevie. A woman sitting next to him stood up suddenly, grabbed her little boy's hand and dragged him to the next carriage. This had the effect of shaming us into sullen silence. The rest of the journey I stared out the window, telling myself not to hope, trying not to believe it was possible, trying not to want anything at all.

We got off the train, still not speaking, but just as we reached the exit Stevie put his arm round my waist. Immediately, I relaxed.

'You are going to go, aren't you? To the agency? It doesn't have to be Wednesday. You don't have to take me. Just go.' His voice was low and serious. After my hissy-fit on the train I couldn't tell him that I had never seriously considered not going, that a part of me was afraid of how much I wanted to go.

So all I said was: 'Yes, Stevie, I'm going – on Wednesday. And you're coming too.' I'd never been to London on my own. I'd never been anywhere, much, without Stevie.

We went to McDonald's on the way back to mine. The

bright plastic chairs looked even brighter and more plasticky than usual. I realised I had a headache.

'Let's eat in,' said Stevie, 'dine in style. It's your birthday.' He ordered me a large fish meal, a Sprite, a strawberry milkshake and a doughnut. He had a grilled chicken wrap.

'Better make the most of it. After next week . . .' he grinned, 'you'll probably never be allowed to eat again.'

I wanted to ask him if he thought I really could be a model, but I didn't want to hear the neediness in my voice. So all I said was, 'I've got a bloody awful headache.' Stevie fished an ice-cube out of his Sprite and ran it across my forehead. Cold sticky water ran down my nose.

'Look at you,' he said, 'Jennifer Jones – supermodel.'

2

The first time I saw the Reed twins I nearly knocked them down I was so desperate for a pee. It was their fifteenth birthday and their first day at our school.

Clare said (I think it was Clare), 'Excuse us – this is the girls' toilets,' as they stepped out of my way.

I hissed, 'I am a girl!' and banged the cubicle door shut.

There was a pause, some whispers, and then a soft scratching on the door. 'We're sorry . . . we didn't realise.'

And I never forgave them for it. Because they weren't trying to be horrible. It was a genuine mistake. For a moment, they really did think I was a boy.

They were identical twins but Clare was the pretty one. Her hair was extra swingy, her smile was whiter and there wasn't a boy in the school who wouldn't have climbed over his dying best friend to get to her. They wouldn't have said no to Louise either, but Louise's good looks just made you notice the extra something her sister had. If they'd gone on *X Factor* as a double act, Simon Cowell would have told Clare to go solo.

It wasn't just their prettiness that got to me; it was their height. If you had stood one twin on top of the other they still wouldn't have been as tall as me. OK I'm exaggerating, a bit, but most of the girls and all of the boys in our year towered over their shiny blonde heads. Even Stevie was taller than the Reed twins.

And it wasn't just their height that got to me – it was their niceness. A week before Corinne and Topshop, Clare and Louise came up to me and Stevie at lunchtime and asked us if we were going to Paula Tweedy's party.

'Everyone's going. You must come,' cooed Clare.

'It'll be brilliant, her mum's away and everything,' simpered Louise. I thought: they're trying to include me. But I wasn't going to fall for their 'be-nice-to-the-boy-girl-freak' crap.

'No we're not going,' I snapped, 'we've got better things to do than stand around all night watching Paula puke up Snakebite.'

The twins said, 'Ohh . . .' – it sounded like air escaping from an old squeaky toy – and scampered off as fast as their little legs would take them.

'That was a bit harsh,' said Stevie, quietly. Sometimes he seemed to forget that Clare and Louise were the Princesses of Plastic. We had to resist them. I mean nine times out of ten he was right there with me, resisting them. Princesses of Plastic? He came up with that. I had nothing to feel guilty about.

And it was stupid of the twins to think we might be going to Paula Tweedy's party. Paula hated me. When she spoke to me, which wasn't often, she called me Morticia, or Marilyn (as in Manson, not Monroe, obviously). Even for a Skank she was nasty.

But I would have rather had Paula's nastiness than the twins' pity, any day. Sometimes when you're having a bad day – and there were a lot of bad days at Nowheresville High School – you can stand anything but somebody feeling sorry for you.

We had three days to kill before going to London, to the agency, to see Corinne. I spent Sunday in my bedroom, on my own, flicking through books I'd already read, the DVD humming, unwatched, in the background. My mum banged on my door and shouted (I just about heard her over the roar of the vacuum cleaner), 'Layabout!' I ignored her.

Stevie was at his grandparents' fortieth wedding anniversary buffet do. He was the only person there older than ten and younger than forty, a trauma that left him almost too weak to text. I got just one message all day: THE HORROR.

At school, on Monday, everything went on as usual. Stevie and I sat next to each other in most of our classes, as we always did, and were more or less ignored by the Plastics and the Skanks, as we usually were. There was no furtive under-the-desk texting (or no more than usual) and we didn't do anything cute like huddle together at lunchtime and squeal with excitement.

I was afraid that if we talked about it – me being a model

– it would jinx it. Meeting Corinne in Topshop was like a scene from a film; it was stupid to go on about it as though it were real life.

But I could tell Stevie was thinking about Saturday, and what might happen on Wednesday. His head wasn't in school, any more than mine was. All the annoying little tics he does when he's just mildly bored (foot tapping, fiddling with a biro, sticking his hand up in class and yelling, 'I know! I know!' when he hasn't got a clue) were gone. He seemed quieter than usual.

Even in art, where Stevie was the only boy and a total star – a Billy Elliott in the middle of us no-talent girls – he was distracted. His clay model of a horse – which had been coming along quite nicely for several weeks – suddenly took a turn for the worse. By the end of the lesson Stevie's aimless hacking had turned it into a deformed donkey. There were bits of mane and tail dropping off.

Miss Jenkins seemed to think he had done it on purpose – her one talented pupil turning rubbish, like the rest of us. She picked up a clay tail and waved it at him, sadly: 'Why, Stevie? Why?'

'Dunno, miss,' said Stevie. Sometimes he could be just like any other boy.

We went to Stevie's place after school. His six-year-old kid brother opened the door.

'Hi, Jimmy,' I said.

'You've got to make me my dinner,' said Jimmy to Stevie.

13

I knew what this meant: their mum was working lates and their dad was doing whatever their dad did when he disappeared for the night.

'Chicken and chips?' Jimmy nodded. Twenty minutes later the kid was gnawing on pizza, because there wasn't any chicken, in front of *Ice Age 2*. The TV looked different, even bigger, if possible, than the one Stevie's dad had bought two weeks earlier. This one took up an entire wall. 'Yeah, it's home-cinema size, high definition, latest model,' said Stevie. He grabbed my arm: 'C'mon.' We went upstairs to his room.

I sat on the bed. Stevie picked up a tatty folder marked 'Maths revision notes' from a pile of schoolbooks. He opened it and pulled out a gleaming silver Apple powerbook.

'If he can't see it, he might forget he gave it to me.' Stevie's dad was always 'he' or 'him', never 'Dad'. 'If he remembers I've got it, he'll sell it.'

'I thought he never came into your room.'

'So did I until he took my Blackberry. It's a new thing, giving me stuff and then stealing it.'

'Look!' he said, as the screen filled with a beautiful scowling face. 'Focus Management.' Focus looked pretty damn slick – there were video clips of fashion shows and a great picture gallery of Francine Hope's magazine covers and advertising campaigns. But the website didn't tell you anything useful about joining Focus or being a model.

We spent hours looking at dozens of modelling websites and none of them – not even howtobeamodel.com – gave us any idea what to expect on Wednesday. Some said age and weight were no barrier to a career in modelling. Quite a few promised to launch your career in return for a modest fee of several hundred pounds to cover 'portfolio costs and administration'.

'Do you think Corinne will expect me to pay?' I asked Stevie.

'Nooo,' he said. 'Don't be stupid.' And then, 'God, do you think she might?'

It was a relief when Jimmy interrupted us. The door creaked open and he tottered a couple of steps forward. He looked a bit crumpled, like he was about to cry, and oddly babyish. It must have been about 11 p.m.

'Ah, Jimmy. Sorry, mate, sorry, let's get you to bed.' Stevie picked Jimmy up and carried him to his room. I heard their voices murmuring together. It was a nice sound but it made me feel sad. Like I shouldn't be there to hear it. I wrote a note for Stevie ('Gone home – see you in school. x'), left it on the laptop keyboard, and let myself out.

I woke up on Tuesday feeling a lot better. We'd got ourselves into a state with all the crappy websites. That was all. Corinne was nice. She discovered Francine Hope at Heathrow. When I was famous everybody would know how Corrine spotted me in Topshop. (I was right about that.) Tomorrow was going to be OK. It was going to be brilliant.

Stevie barely spoke in class, and I didn't hear a word the teachers said. I was back in a dream world. In biology I imagined Miss McAllister flicking through a glossy magazine in the staff room and seeing me on the cover and being really impressed. I saw her calling all the other teachers over and saying, 'I used to teach that girl – I knew she'd go far'. I quite liked Miss McAllister. She acted as if plants and cells and stuff were really interesting and because of her sometimes they were. And she was one of the few teachers who treated Clare and Louise like they were nothing special. Miss McAllister was cool.

When the bell went Dwayne Smith was the first one out of his seat. He hung around until Clare and Louise reached the door and then he held it open for them. Dwayne had only recently been let back into school (there'd been an incident with a cigarette lighter and a teacher's scarf) but he was the best-looking boy in our year and everybody fancied him. He didn't usually make any effort to get girls because he didn't have to; they just sort of attached themselves to him until he got bored and shook them off. But here he was, putting on a show for the twins. They walked under his arm, giggling. Dwayne said, 'Ladies,' in a funny deep voice, like he'd just done it for a joke, but his face was bright red.

'How come nobody bullies them?' said Stevie as we followed the twins out into the corridor. We walked slowly behind them, keeping a safe distance from their perkiness, like it was infectious. 'I'm serious. Why don't the hard-faced Skanks in our class just kill them?' He shook his head at the world's foolishness.

'Because the boys would kill the Skanks,' I said, though

I wasn't sure if that was it, really. Everybody got a bit funny around Clare and Louise, even the girls. I once saw Leanne Cody – a girl so hard she said getting an ASBO was 'gay' – reach over to Clare in the middle of an English test and stroke her hair. It was as though everybody who didn't want to shag them wanted to keep them as pets. Only Stevie and me were immune.

As Clare and Louise climbed the stairs at the end of the corridor and disappeared I wondered if they would be pleased for me if they knew about this whole modelling thing. I had a feeling they would.

'I bet when you're a model on the cover of *Vogue* they'll throw you a party,' whispered Stevie in my ear, 'you know, to celebrate. They're so . . . nice.' Normally I would have resented any sign of his weakening towards the Princesses of Plastic but I decided to let this go. Because he'd said, 'when you're a model' – he'd said 'when', like it was a sure thing.

We were going to London – tomorrow – and we were going to leave the Skanks and the Reed twins and everybody we knew behind us. And everything was going to change.

3

Of course on Wednesday morning we were jumpy and strung out and totally nervous. We didn't worry about skipping school though. There was a nasty stomach bug going round, and we'd agreed we would both have it for the day. Stevie wrote sick notes from our mums on the train to London. I always told him he would have made a great forger. We bunked off a couple of times a term and, thanks to Stevie's notes, never got caught.

Stevie was quite strict about not overusing his forgery skills. We only took a sickie when we had a really good reason – like on his sixteenth birthday when he wanted to celebrate by working through an *Ugly Betty* box set.

Several of the Skanks were hard-core, committed escapees. Paula Tweedy and her best mate Janine were basically in part-time education. Nobody could stop them. When the school gates were locked and they felt the urge to go, they would just climb over the security fence. It would have taken electrified barbed wire to stop them, and maybe armed guards with tracker dogs.

They were brilliant at getting out of school but they

never seemed to do anything that great with all their free time. Just the usual stuff: robbing make-up from Superdrug; drinking lager in the kiddies' playground behind the shopping mall; getting caught by the truancy officers and being dragged to the police station and then, finally, back to school. 'Lame,' Stevie called Paula and Janine, 'totally sad, predictable and lame.'

'This is genius,' he said. 'It must be the best reason ever for bunking off school.'

'Yeah,' I said, 'it must.' We grinned at each other and for a moment I stopped feeling nervous and a surge of pure excitement went through me.

Once we got to London it took us about an hour to find the agency. It should have only taken thirty minutes to get to Covent Garden but we got off at the wrong tube stop and then we started bickering about the best route to take. We only stopped arguing when we found ourselves in the reception at Focus.

It was smaller than I'd expected – though until we got there I didn't know I'd been expecting anything – and intensely, harshly white. It made me want to rub my eyes. Rows of framed photos behind the reception desk provided the only colour: blondes, brunettes, black girls, Asian girls. They all looked weirdly the same – apart from Francine Hope. There must have been about ten of her, mostly magazine covers; she kind of jumped out at you.

'Yes?' said the receptionist. I found out later her name

was Madeleine, and she was the only receptionist in the model agency world who actually wanted to be a receptionist and not an agent or a magazine editor or a model. 'I just like working the front desk,' she told me months later at the agency's Christmas party, 'it's my thing. It soothes me. Everything else you can do in modelling is just – crazy.' On that first day, though, Madeleine was just a gorgeous black girl wearing headphones. I thought she was better looking than some of the girls in the framed pictures.

'Have you an appointment?' she said. I expected Stevie to take over like he usually did, but he just stood there – mute.

'Erm, yes, we're here to see Corinne,' I said, 'we're a bit late. Really sorry – we got lost . . .'

'Don't worry, you're here now,' said Madeleine. She took our names, buzzed Corinne, and told us to go the first floor and take a right. We found Corinne standing outside her office, waiting.

'I'm so glad you came,' she said, and she put her hand out and sort of rubbed my arm. I got to know that gesture well over the next two years; she always did it when she was pleased to see you, or she wanted to make you feel better. When she didn't do it it meant she was seriously pissed off. Not getting the arm rub from Corinne was worse than being bawled out by anyone else in the agency.

She showed us into her office and we sat down on huge, amazingly comfortable purple chairs. It was like getting a whole body hug.

'Yes, I know – they're great to sit in, aren't they?' said

Corinne. 'I've had models fall asleep in those chairs.'

Models. There it was. The reason why we were here.

'I'm sure there must be lots you'd like to ask me, but let me just explain first why you are here . . .'

'Is she going to have to pay?' said Stevie. For a moment I had no idea what he meant, I was just horrified at the rude way he had spoken to Corinne. It was like a dog waking from a deep sleep and barking. Corinne looked mystified.

'Pay?' she said.

'Yeah – you know, to join the agency. Fees for administration costs and, er, her portfolio.' Then I remembered our internet search and all those 'pay us and we'll make you a model' dodgy-looking websites. It seemed unlikely that Corinne would appreciate Focus being compared to the likes of www.Be-A-Hot-Model.com. I could hardly breathe I was so embarrassed. Bloody Stevie and his great big mouth.

'Oh I see what you mean. No – absolutely not,' said Corinne. She didn't look at all put out. 'No reputable agency would charge a girl for being on their books. Everything we spend on Jen – photography fees, travel, accommodation, everything she needs to get started – will be set against her future earnings. That means,' she turned to me, 'you'll pay us back when you start earning. And then of course there is our twenty per cent commission on the work we secure for you. But you don't have to give us any money now. Any agency that takes money off a girl up front, they're just con artists.'

This was quite a relief, because I didn't have any money.

But me being me, I had to start worrying about something else, straightaway.

I still couldn't quite believe that Corinne was serious. At that moment I wouldn't have been surprised if the whole thing was a set-up for some particularly cruel reality TV show. You know – 'Mingers Who Think They Look Like Models'. So I went out of my way to point out to Corinne that I was, in fact, a total moose.

'So, er, what made you notice me in Topshop? I mean I'm not pretty. Nobody has ever said I'm pretty. I know how I look and it's . . . not pretty.'

Corinne smiled. Her smile was dazzling. 'You don't have to be pretty to be a model. There are a lot of pretty girls who could never be models. It takes a lot more: a face that the camera loves, a personality that can bring clothes to life. When I saw you in Topshop you were so . . . striking . . . I knew I had to get a closer look. We've only just met, Jen, but I have a feeling you've got it all.

'And you're right, Jen, you're not pretty. But you are beautiful. And a beauty like yours doesn't come along very often.'

I went bright red. I don't often blush but when I do it's horribly obvious – flares go off in my cheeks. It felt like blood vessels might actually be bursting. Corinne got up and walked to the water cooler in the corner of her office. She filled a plastic cup, came back and handed it to me.

'Here, drink this.'

I gulped the water down noisily. Corinne smiled. 'Better?'

I nodded.

'Good. Now, can you do something for me?' I nodded again. Her voice was low and soothing. 'Just tuck your hair behind your ears and turn your face to the right – yes, like that – towards the window.' I did exactly as I was told. If she had asked me to jump out of the window I might have done that too. It was like being stroked, hypnotised. I heard a drawer open – and then a click. I turned to see Corinne holding the biggest camera I'd ever seen in my life. She looked at the screen at the back of the camera and then said, so quietly I could hardly hear her, 'Yes, I knew it.' She pushed the camera across the desk, towards me. I picked it up; I can remember the weight of it my hands, and how scared I was that I might drop it.

'Look, Jen – can you see what I see?' I stared at the screen and saw me – or somebody who had to be me – with her hair scraped behind her ears. I never usually let myself be photographed in profile because I didn't like my nose; but in Corinne's picture, I had to admit, the nose didn't look so bad.

'You have amazing bone structure, wonderfully clean lines.'

I felt the heat in my cheeks building again. Corinne, with her usual tact, didn't say anything more about my clean lines and rare beauty. She moved on to safer ground.

'So tell me, Jen, are you interested in fashion? You look as though you are. That outfit you're wearing' – it was a long, ankle-length black skirt, with lace-up ankle boots and a short white wool jacket with a huge pointy collar – 'it's fabulous.'

Now, usually, nobody ever asked me about my clothes. Or

rather, they did, but the question was usually along the lines of did-you-steal-that-off-a-granny-it's-bloody-horrible? But here was a real-life fashion expert, telling me my clothes were 'fabulous'. It was like she'd turned on a tap: all this stuff just poured out of me.

'I love clothes! I've always loved them – since I was a little girl. I used to dress up in my mum's high heels . . .'

'Yeah, I used to do that too,' said Stevie.

'. . . and I read all the fashion magazines and I sort of copy ideas and then I buy stuff from charity shops – this jacket it's from Oxfam, you know, "vintage" – and adapt it. And sometimes I think I've put together something really nice. But I don't know if it is nice, really, cos only Stevie likes the way I dress. And my mum says I'll never get a boyfriend, going out looking the way I do.' At the end of this I stopped because I needed to breathe. I was pleased that I'd managed to use the word 'vintage'; I knew it was fashion-speak for 'second-hand'.

'Well, Stevie has great taste – you look amazing,' said Corinne. Stevie beamed. 'And you've got plenty of time for boys.'

And then she opened a drawer in her desk and pulled out a thick folder.

'Right, let's get the basics out of the way.'

For the next half hour or so, Corinne talked me through the 'basics'. She showed me the kind of contract I would be asked to sign. She explained that the agency would try to book jobs for the school holidays. They would take me out of school as little as possible; she said this like it was a good thing.

'When you are eighteen, if everything is going well, you can leave school and come and work for us full-time, it will be your choice. But we don't want girls to throw away their chance of an education. It's good to have an insurance policy in this business. Even the most successful model's career is short. And – though I have every confidence in you – there are no guarantees. You have to keep your head, Jen. It's a tough world out there.'

I nodded because I couldn't think of anything to say. She could have said 'the modelling world is made of cheese and exists in outer space – watch out for the little green men' and I would probably still have nodded. I'd been reading fashion magazines since I was eleven but I knew nothing, absolutely nothing, about this new 'world'. And then she said something that really worried me.

'Of course, before we take you on we will need to get your parents' permission.'

I swallowed, hard.

'There's just my mum.'

'OK, your mum then. I'd like to meet her and have a chat, make sure she understands what this involves, and that she supports you becoming a model. You did tell her you were coming here today, didn't you?'

'Er . . .'

'Oh God yes!' yelped Stevie.

'And of course your mum will probably want her lawyer to check the contract.'

The thought of my mum meeting Corinne, being in the same room as Corinne, was horrible. It hadn't occurred to me that I would have to tell her. This was bad news. Almost as bad as the news that I would have to stay at school for another two years.

I guess I thought that becoming a model would be a bit like running away to join the circus: big, dramatic, final. One day you're living your old dull life and the next you're in a sparkly leotard, walking the tightrope. But here was Corinne, telling me it was going to be a bit more complicated. She was right, of course.

But now I come to think about it maybe I wasn't so far off the mark. Modelling like walking a tightrope? Yeah. It's exactly like that.

'Don't worry about your mum,' said Stevie. We were walking down Long Acre, towards Leicester Square tube. 'We can handle her.'

I was clutching a bag full of paperwork Corinne had given me to show my mum. We were supposed to come back in a week – mother and daughter together – to get me formally signed up to the agency.

'What if she tries to stop me?' I said.

'She won't.' He put his arm round my waist.

'She might.'

'No, she won't.'

'What makes you so sure?'

'Because she's sick of your Aunt Pat queening it over her with her perfect house, and her perfect husband and her perfect bloody daughter. Think about it – think how much fun she will have telling her sister that you are going to be a model. Aunt Pat will probably be sick on the spot.'

I giggled. Maybe Stevie was right. Aunt Pat was convinced her daughter, my cousin Bethany (AKA Little Miss Twinkletoes), was a raving beauty. She had a toe-curling habit of saying things like 'That Kate Moss is nothing next to our Bethany,' in front of Bethany.

'Sometimes I think you understand my mum a lot better than I do.'

'Of course I do,' said Stevie, 'I'm much smarter than you. Oh look – H&M! Shall we?'

'Let's,' I said.

We spent the next hour trawling through the rails and trying on clothes without bothering to go into the changing rooms. It was fun. Nobody seemed to mind until Stevie fell into an accessories display while pulling on a pair of trousers over his skinny jeans. Then we were politely asked to leave. We were still laughing when we got on to the tube. I forgot why we had come to London. It was as if hanging out with Stevie was all there was, all there needed to be.

That's the last time I remember life being like that. Just me and Stevie. It was also the last time I was, in my own freaky way, just an ordinary teenager.

4

Stevie was right about my mum. She didn't exactly jump for joy – in fact she said, 'You – a model? Are they sure?' – but she didn't try to stop me either.

I must have looked relieved – too relieved – when she said she'd come up to London and meet Corinne, because she gave me a sharp look.

'You don't think much of me, do you, Jennifer? Believe it or not, I want you to make something of yourself. I'd never try to stop you.'

'I know you wouldn't . . . really,' but we both knew I was lying.

I was worried she would show me up in front of Corinne. But on the day she was fine. Very well behaved, in fact. She wore a dull but not hideous suit, shook Corinne's hand, said, 'It's a very good opportunity for Jennifer,' and signed on the dotted line. I couldn't have asked for more.

When we got home I put the kettle on. Mum didn't take her coat off and she didn't sit down. She followed me into the kitchen and stood there, watching me make tea.

'Well, Jennifer, I suppose you'll be off my hands soon.' I

thought: I'm only sixteen and you can't wait to get rid of me. And then she surprised me.

'Be a good girl. Make me proud,' and she hugged me, hard. I was just about to hug her back when she pushed me away. For a small woman, my mum's incredibly strong. Her eyes were shining.

'Never mind the tea,' she said, heading for the door, 'I'm popping out. Must tell your Aunt Pat the good news.'

The newspapers and fashion magazines called me an overnight sensation. You've probably seen the headlines: *The Super-fast rise of the supermodel from Nowhere*, and my personal favourite, *From classroom to catwalk in 60 seconds*.

Actually it took about three months. Apparently this is a ridiculously short time to make it in fashion – even Kate Moss earned peanuts for a few years before she achieved world domination. But three months didn't feel 'overnight' to me. Three months is a long time when you're leading a double life.

Of course my mum knew about my trips to London, but she never really asked me about them. Sometimes she would look up from the TV when I got back and say, 'How's that Corinne? Looking after you all right?' Or if she was in a bad mood she wouldn't bother looking up. But she didn't give me any grief.

I'd always had trouble deciding what was worse: school or home. But now there was no contest. School was far scarier than home. School had to be kept in the dark. The thought of one of the Skanks finding out that the class freak was trying to be a model was deeply, awesomely frightening. I couldn't quite imagine what form my public humiliation would take but I knew it would involve a lot more than name-calling. 'Maybe they'll creep up behind you in a corridor and cut off your hair!' suggested Stevie. 'You know – attack your looks and ruin your career. Oh don't look at me like that – I'm kidding!'

As it happened, getting my hair cut probably made my career. It was Corinne who suggested a radical new look.

'You know, Jen, I don't think this is working for you.' She picked up a hank of my hair, lifting it an inch or two off my shoulders, and rubbed it between her fingers, like a dressmaker choosing fabric. I flinched because, back then, I wasn't used to being touched. She dropped the hair and took a step or two back, to get a better look.

'No, it has to go; it's hiding you. We need to show those bones.' It was only my second visit to the agency. My long hair was the only girly thing about me. I didn't want to lose it. I wished Stevie was with me but he was at home, looking after his little brother who had a cold. (I said that maybe his mum could look after Jimmy for a change, but he wasn't going to get into that. 'You'll be OK. And it's you Corinne wants to see, not me.' Fine, I'd said. Fine.)

'Don't look so worried, Jen,' said Corinne. 'You can trust me. I'm going to send you to Mark – he cuts Francine's hair – he's one of the best in town.' Since Francine had hair down to her waist I wasn't much comforted by this. Super-stylist Mark clearly didn't get to do a lot of cutting when he was working on Francine. But I did trust Corinne. If she said my hair wasn't doing me any favours, then maybe it wasn't.

Two hours later I was sitting in a salon in Soho with Mark's scissors flying through my hair. (It turned out Corinne had already made the appointment for me. 'I didn't want to frighten you off by telling you in advance,' she said, as she pushed me gently out of her office.)

There were two other girls from the agency sitting in the chairs next to me, having their hair cut by Mark's assistants. I didn't want to see what was happening to my hair in case I started crying like a big baby, so I watched the other girls out of the corner of my eye. There was a delicate-looking blonde with big green eyes and a cute button nose on my right-hand side. She looked as much like a kitten as it is possible to look without actually being one. When she sat down she had long beautiful hair and when the cut was finished she still had long beautiful hair. The other girl went from shoulder-length brunette to chin-length redhead.

'Oh God, what have you done, you cow?' said the brand-new redhead. 'My boyfriend will kill me! I look like a right dog,' and she started to cry, great gulping, angry sobs. I thought she looked great but I didn't have the nerve to tell her.

Mark was obviously used to this kind of drama. 'Step aside,' he said to his assistant. He gripped the redhead's shoulders. 'Don't you dare insult my staff. You should be thanking her. Your old cut was a high street hatchet job.

Now you look like a model. Your boyfriend won't be able to keep his hands off you. If he doesn't fancy you with this cut, dump him. I'll shag you myself.' She stopped crying. Then she looked in the mirror and started sniffling again.

'Look at Jen,' said Mark, swinging her chair round so she was pointed straight at me, 'she's lost about two feet of hair – she's practically Edie Sedgwick – and she's not crying. She's a professional.' It was only then that I realised my cut was finished.

I looked in the mirror.

I'm not going to exaggerate and say I saw a complete stranger looking back; it was more like seeing a long-lost twin sister. It was short, very short. But the cut wasn't about hair; the girl in the mirror didn't have a great haircut – she had a great face. I was expecting cheekbones – Corinne had said the cut would show off my bones – and yes, there they were. But the big news was my eyes: I noticed for the first time that they were sort of almond-shaped; even the hazel colour seemed stronger, darker, than before.

I smiled. It was like a lot of worry and tension – about losing my long hair, about being here without Stevie – just fell off me.

'It's great. It's really great. Thank you.'

'Good girl,' said Mark. 'You're welcome. Now get out of here, the three of you, and start paying Focus back for these haircuts. It's time to go to work.'

5

Going to work, when you're a model, isn't just a matter of turning up and clocking in. It's not like working in an office, or being at school. You have to be picked – booked – for everything that you do. Just getting work is a job in itself.

During my first month with Focus I took several days off school to go to London. Corinne sorted it out with the head teacher, so I didn't need Stevie's forgery skills to explain my absences. It was like having a licence to bunk off. The teachers must have been sworn to secrecy; I got a few odd looks but they didn't drop any clangers. There were no 'Welcome back Jennifer, everybody – she's been off to London to be a model!' type comments.

None of my fellow pupils, apart from Stevie, even seemed to notice I was gone. The haircut, of course, made an impression. But the comments it provoked ('Given up trying to look like a girl, Jen?'/'You look like a right lez') quickly ran out of steam. I was relieved and, I admit, a tiny bit put out: it seemed they didn't care enough about me to make my life a misery.

'Even the Skanks have other things on their minds,' said

Stevie, as we arrived at school one wet, cold morning. 'You know what their schedules are like: court appearances, pregnancy scares, planning the next post office heist. It's not all about you. Don't ask me to sympathise because the people you hate are not beating you up. Besides, you get to visit Planet Fashion whenever you like. But for me – this is my world.' He waved his hand. It was a gesture that took in the entire school: the grey playground where everybody just stood around texting; the main school building, with its green and brown paintwork, squatting like a malignant toad; the temporary classrooms that creaked and groaned in stormy weather.

Stevie didn't get to go to London with me, not after that first time at the agency. The licence to bunk off didn't apply to him. I asked Corinne if he could come with me on some of my castings but she said turning up with a mate wouldn't make the right impression. 'Only really young models have chaperones,' she added, 'and chaperones are responsible adults, not friends. Sorry, Jen – I'm afraid there are a lot of things you will have to do on your own. It gets easier, honest.' We were speaking on the phone so I didn't get the arm rub, but I could hear it in her voice. I still felt stupid for having asked.

Because he wasn't allowed to come with me to 'Planet Fashion', Stevie couldn't know what it was like. I tried telling him, but I got the feeling he thought I was leaving stuff out. I don't think he really believed that it was quite as un-glamorous as I said it was.

* * *

My first casting was for a new range of organic herbal shampoos. I was surprised when Corinne said she was putting me up for it.

'Shampoo? Really? But I've hardly got any hair now.'

'You do have hair, and it's fabulous – and the client is looking for at least three girls with very different styles. I'm also sending Sophie.'

'Sophie?'

'Yes, you know, the blonde girl. She was at Mark's getting her hair cut, same time as you.' I remembered: kitten-face.

'So what do I have to do?'

'Just turn up with clean hair. And don't be late.'

I was late. I still hadn't developed a sense of direction or got to grips with the underground system. When I was a kid I yearned for big city life the way other little girls want a pony. But my fantasies never involved standing in a packed tube carriage with someone's face pressed into my bony chest, or wandering the streets hopelessly lost and too scared to ask for directions. Everybody who looked sane was clearly in too much of a hurry to be interrupted; anyone who could be interrupted would probably give me directions and then ask for something in return, like my liver.

By the time I made it to the casting – at the hair company's headquarters near Liverpool Street – I was in such a panic that my hair was clamped to my head with sweat. Which meant I was forty minutes late with dirty-looking hair.

I spluttered out my apologies to the woman at reception but she just raised an eyebrow and said, as if speaking to someone else, 'Good grief. Another one. It's madness.'

There must have been a hundred girls up for the organic hair range ad. And we were all crammed into a badly lit, airless room in the basement of the building. All the long blondes were in the top third of the room, the short brunettes were in the middle, and the shoulder-length redheads were in the bottom third. It was like a school assembly, organised by a colour-obsessed madman. I made my way into the middle section, found an empty seat, and sat down.

Right at the top of the room, just a few inches from the first line of blondes, was a small platform with three men in suits and two much younger guys, both in sleek leather jackets. I couldn't hear what they were saying over the chatter of a hundred bored girls, but the body language didn't look good. Leather jacket number one had his head thrown back and was staring at the ceiling; leather jacket number two was shaking his head as though he couldn't believe what he had to put with up; and the three suits looked about ready to exchange punches. There was finger pointing and everything – real playground stuff from middle-aged men.

Suddenly one of the suits stormed out. And, quite suddenly, it was down to business.

'OK, girls, apologies for the delay. Just had to sort out a few creative differences. We're ready for you now,' said leather jacket number two. He was on his feet and speaking into a microphone. 'My name's Martin, I'm from the advertising agency which will be running the campaign. And this is Alfie, the campaign's photographer,' he waved his arm towards leather jacket number one, 'and these gentleman . . .' he gestured towards the suits, 'are here to represent the client, Nature's Own. You've got to impress us all.

'We need three girls for the campaign – a blonde, a brunette and a redhead. In a minute Alfie and I will come down and have a closer look at you. We're going to ask you all to stand up, one row at a time. If we touch you on the shoulder please make your way to the platform. Try to relax. This isn't just about great hair – it's about great personality.'

I wondered how I was supposed to show my personality while standing silently in a line. I noticed quite a few of the girls flicking their hair and touching up their lip-gloss. When the leather jackets reached the girl on my right she pushed her chest so far forward, I swear I heard something crack; then she drawled, 'Hi, guys.' They walked straight past her – and stopped in front of me. My heart was thumping. At school I never got picked for anything. Not team sports, not the school play, nothing. And I didn't get picked for this either.

'She has a great look. Yes?' said the photographer.

'Yes,' said the advertising guy. 'But not for this client. Too fashion.' They moved on.

All the rejected girls had to sit and wait until the chosen

ones were on the platform. Then the advertising guy thanked us and asked us to leave. As I filed out I glanced round and looked at the twenty or so girls who had made it on to the platform. Sophie was among them, her baby blonde, almost white hair making the other blondes looks mousy. She was gazing at the exit as though she wanted to go too; I guess that's why she saw me. She lifted her hand and waved. I waved back. It was, oddly, rather comforting. We'd never spoken but at least we recognised each other.

As I walked out of the building I found myself hoping that Sophie would get the job.

For the next couple of weeks I went to school, did my homework, and hung out with Stevie. I had to take the odd morning or afternoon off school to go to castings or 'go-sees' but it wasn't exactly a hectic schedule. I didn't understand why I was knackered.

The go-sees were so casual they were insulting. A lot of the time there wasn't even a particular job on offer. I just had to turn up, present my 'book' – a portfolio of my best pictures – to the photographer or magazine editor, and hope they would keep me in mind if something came up.

My 'book' was pretty pathetic. Since I'd never actually had a job, it was made up of basic shots of me in various poses: close-ups in profile and full face; and body shots standing, seated and lying down. During the shoot – in a draughty studio just two minutes round the corner from the Focus office – I'd got the feeling that the photographer was in a bad mood, or maybe he just didn't like the way I looked. He said, 'Great, yeah, great,' in a flat toneless voice as he snapped away, and then (with unmistakable feeling) 'No! Not like that!' whenever I did something he particularly hated. I tensed up and it showed in the photos. They made me look like a stroppy beanpole. Which, of course, is just what I was.

Every time I had to show my book, I felt a bit ashamed. I wanted to say, I can do better – really, I can. I was eager to please, but it was more than that. I was ambitious. I wanted to work. I wanted to get booked for everything, and do it brilliantly. Maybe I also wanted to make my mum proud.

Go-sees at magazine offices were the worst. Sometimes a fashion editor or stylist would ask to see my walk; and then I'd have to parade myself past their desk, in front of people working on computers, busy doing their real jobs. No one ever tells you on the spot whether they intend to use you – they go through your agent – so however badly I thought it went, I always hoped.

The hope was exhausting; it would be with me on the train going home, it would keep me awake at night and follow me to school the next day. And then Corinne would phone and say no, no bookings this time, but never mind because she had another go-see organised for tomorrow. And then the whole cycle – hope followed by disappointment – would start up again.

Just when I thought my modelling career had stalled before it began, Corinne phoned and said she was sending me on a 'blitz': ten go-sees in one day. It was more than I'd clocked up in the previous fortnight. 'We've got to get your face out there – let people know you exist,' said Corinne. 'It'll be tough but if you're really cut out for this business, you'll enjoy it. I want to hear good things about you, Jen. Don't let me down.'

I set out on the 7 a.m. commuter train into London, determined to get it right. Corinne said the girls who got booked most often were enthusiastic and easy – as in easy to work with. At each go-see I had just a few minutes to show my enthusiasm, and easiness.

I smiled, shook hands, said I felt 'great' as if I meant it, and walked up and down in magazine offices and photographers' studios with my hand on my hip trying to look sexy. When they handed my book back to me I said, 'Thank you, it's been so nice meeting you,' like it had been the thrill of my life. It made a difference. I got three really positive comments: 'You have great skin, really clear. I can see you in a skincare commercial'; 'You have fantastic bones. How is Corinne by the way?'; and 'What a strong look you have – so original.'

That night, in the bathroom at home, I took off my shoes and mopped the insides with cotton wool; they were smeared with blood. I'd thought high heels would make me look more elegant, more like a model. Lying in the bath, I watched my swollen toes peeking through the suds. I was happy. I knew I had done well. I knew I would get a job.

Two days later, Corinne called me and said she'd had

some fantastic feedback from my go-sees. But no, nobody wanted to book me for a job, not at the moment.

'Did Sophie get the shampoo ad?' I said. 'I mean, they chose her, out of all those girls, I saw her. Did she get it?'

'Yes, Jen, she did,' said Corinne, gently. 'Sophie has the right look for that job – that's all it is you know. It will happen for you too.'

I said I was pleased for Sophie, and I was. Then I switched off my phone for the first time in a month, and burst into tears.

6

'I think it's time you met Madja.' Corinne seemed to think I knew who Madja was. The name was familiar. I had an uncomfortable feeling that I really should have known who she was.

'Madja likes to take a personal interest in all our most promising new girls.' Clearly being introduced to this Madja person was some sort of honour. I thought briefly about faking delight and then decided not to risk it.

'Sorry, but who is Madja?'

'Madja set up Focus in the 1980s. She made it into one of the most cutting-edge agencies in Europe – and back then London agencies were nowhere. It was all about Paris and New York. She's a legend. If Madja likes you it will make a huge difference to your career. She knows everybody who is anybody. She can get a top photographer to try out a new girl, as a personal favour.' I could do with all the favours I could get, I thought, grimly. But as usual, I was suspicious of any bit of good fortune coming my way.

'Why would she want to see me? It's been nearly two

months and I haven't got a single booking. I don't think that makes me promising.'

Corinne looked, I thought, a tiny bit irritated by this remark. 'Jen, you have to stop being so down on yourself. I'm not worried that you haven't worked yet – and neither should you be. Some of the best girls in the world had knock-backs when they were starting out. It goes with the territory. When Kate Moss was new on the scene everybody thought she was too short, and too ordinary, to make it big. Her look, at the time, was quite unusual. So is yours. When you have a new look it can take a while for people to "get" it. You need to work hard, and be patient. And you need to grab every chance that comes your way with both hands – not push it away.'

I fought the urge to apologise for being negative; saying sorry would just be another form of being down on myself. Corinne was looking for something else from me.

'So when can I meet Madja?'

Corinne smiled. 'Right now.'

Corinne sorted out my hair. But it was Madja who made sure I could walk. One-step-in-front-of-the-other/gets-you-from-A-to-B type walking is for civilians. Model walking is in a whole different class; it's the difference between your boyfriend dancing at his big sister's wedding and, say, Justin Timberlake performing at the MTV Music Europe Awards. I did not know this. I thought all I'd have to do, in the unlikely event that any designer ever put me on a catwalk, was prance up and down with one hand on my hip, looking snooty. Madja set me straight.

'We're going to launch you at the shows next month.' She ground her cigarette into an ashtray shaped like a chimpanzee's hand. Imagine a scientist's laboratory after the circus has passed through – that's Madja's office: white walls, white floor, white furniture and over it all a sort of luridly coloured, mainly animal-printed, rubble; even her desk-height bin – the final resting place of old cigarettes – is made out of faux leopard skin; at least I hope it's faux. If someone told me Madja was accessorising her office with endangered species, frankly, I would not be surprised.

'The shows?' I said.

'Yes, dearie – a little thing called London Fashion Week.' She gave me a look that reminded me powerfully of my Year Twelve maths teacher Miss Perry. It was a look that said your ignorance is appalling but I expected no better. I wished Corinne was with me. But she'd only stayed a couple of minutes, cooed, 'Be gentle with her, Madja darling,' and scarpered.

'You are sooo London,' drawled Madja, cocking her head to one side, her heavily kohled eyes all over me. 'There are two or three designers who should just eat you up. You could create quite a buzz. You might even be *a moment.*'

'That's brilliant,' I said, wondering what I would have to do to be a moment. 'Er, thanks.'

'Well, if we can't get you cast in London then God help you in Paris.' I didn't like the suggestion that Paris wasn't for the likes of me. I'd had that all my life. At seven I got demoted from angel to shepherd in my primary school nativity play because the headmistress thought black hair wasn't angelic. At thirteen I was too tall to be a bridesmaid at Aunt Pat's wedding. ('We can't have you looking down on the groom now, can we?' said Aunt Pat, scrubbing my tear-stained snotty face with a hanky. 'Don't be selfish. Think about the photos.')

Still, at least I had the right look for London, the coolest fashion town in the world, where I was going to be *launched* and have a *moment*. There would be flowers and champagne and photographers snapping madly at me, me, me.

'Of course we'll have to do something about your walk.' For the few seconds it took to drag myself back from my catwalk triumph fantasy I actually had no idea what Madja meant. Naturally, I was used to having the piss taken out of me for my six foot height, my hooky nose, my huge size eight feet, my pasty face, and my lank black hair; each feature came with its own specific set of insults. But no one had ever said there was anything wrong with my walk. Until today. I braced myself.

'You're a little round-shouldered, I noticed it straightaway when you came into my office, and you take small steps for a girl your height. The overall effect is sheepish. Walk like that on a runway and you'll get nowhere.'

I was stung. And angry. 'I wouldn't walk like that on a catwalk – I mean *runway*. I would be completely different. It's not fair to judge me on the basis of the five steps it took to get me from the door to this chair.' Immediately, I wished I had kept my mouth shut. I was picking a fight with the boss of Focus.

'Really?' said Madja. 'Well I'm glad to see you've got some spirit. Let's see what you can do. Get up and walk the length of this office – from the filing cabinet to the water cooler. Pretend you're parading in front of the world's press, with a twenty thousand dollar frock on your back.'

I was horrified. 'Now?'

'Yes, dearie, now.'

I did as I was told. When I sat down again I didn't need to look at Madja's face to know that my walk had been a disaster. I'd tried to compensate for my round shoulders by leaning back and sticking my nose in the air; I could hardly see where I was going and my steps were so huge I'd misjudged the turn and kicked the filing cabinet.

'That was horrible, dear, quite horrible,' said Madja. 'But there's no need to look so worried. I've seen worse. It's nothing that can't be fixed. I'm sending you to Jeannie. Jeannie will sort you out. Complete bloody miracle worker is Jeannie. She could turn a carthorse into a ballerina.'

'Good,' I said. 'Brilliant.'

Three hours, two tubes and one bus ride later I found myself standing outside a factory in the East End. I knew this because the sign on the massive black door in front of me said 'East End Factory'. I was one hour late and panting hard. I pressed a buzzer marked '4th Floor Jeannie'.

'Come up or sod off,' said a deep male voice. American, I thought.

Fighting the urge to run away, I squeaked, 'Sorry, but is Jeannie there please?'

'Who wants her?' I gave my name.

'Oh, one of Madja's. Why didn't you say? You're late.' The door sprang open and I lurched forward on to a damp cement floor. Picking myself up and brushing down my dirty-wash jeans (now with added, genuine dirt) I looked around to see who, this time, had witnessed me making a prat of myself. But there was no one.

I was standing in a dimly lit corridor with nothing to see except a row of padlocked doors to the right and, straight in front of me, an old-fashioned lift with a concertina metal grill. I wondered where the factory workers had gone and if anything actually got made here.

I got into the lift; it felt like a cage. The effort involved in hauling the metal grill shut, and the grinding industrial noise as it cranked into life, was oddly comforting. I stepped out of the lift at the fourth floor, straight into a huge white room. In the middle of the room was a long raised platform – a runway. I was so startled – I was expecting another corridor, another door – that I forgot to mumble an apology for being late.

'Come over here, chicken, and let Jeannie have a look at you,' said the largest black man I had ever seen in my life. I looked up; in his bare feet Jeannie would have been six inches taller than me. And he was wearing high heels.

Suddenly I got a glimpse of how all those girly-sized girls must have felt when I stood next to them – as if they were in the shadow of a giant flesh skyscraper. I couldn't remember the last time I felt small. It wasn't the relief I thought it would be.

'I see Madja's given me something to work with this time,' said Jeannie. I had no idea whether this was a good or a bad thing but, fortunately, no response seemed to be required. Jeannie was wearing a high-cut sleeveless leotard and a see-though gauzy skirt, slashed to the waist. I tried not to look at his, er, bulges.

'Go sit with the other girls' – what other girls? – 'they're behind you, chicken. Look and learn.'

I sat on a hard white bench next to two blondes and a redhead. One of the blondes was Sophie. It was the second time I'd seen her that day; as I was going into Madja's office she'd been coming out, looking like a rabbit who had narrowly escaped being skinned.

'Hi, Sophie,' I whispered. 'You here too?'

'Hi, Jen.' She smiled; I got a glimpse of small perfectly white teeth.

'Ladies! For the last time – this is how it's done!' Jeannie boomed from the farthest end of the catwalk. Then the music started: *The first time I saw you I knew it was love . . . Cuba!* I didn't recognise the song but the beat was a hammer in my chest; the singer sounded happy but hysterical. I liked it. Jeannie waited (for what I don't know), and then, at some invisible signal, strutted forward, propelled by the music, owning it. His walk was ridiculous, but executed with such steely seriousness that you could not laugh at it. Impossibly long legs jerked and smacked the floor with such force it seemed the floor – or his spindly heels at least – must crack. From the pelvis upwards his body seemed to float through the air. He was ferocious movement and total stillness all at the same time.

I shook my head as though trying to clear water from my ears; I didn't understand what I was seeing. I could not be asked to imitate this – it was crazy.

'You, new girl – it's your turn.' The music had stopped and Jeannie was looming over me, half-smiling. This close up he looked old; he could have been forty.

'What about the others?' I hardly knew my own voice, it had shrunk to a whisper.

'Oh they've shaken their little tushes for Jeannie. It was quite a show. You missed it. You were late.'

I nodded and got up. I walked to the end of the room – my normal creeping walk – climbed the steps up on to the runway and then turned to face Jeannie. From here, the girls all looked the same, even the redhead had merged into the blondes.

'You're in Jeannie's model army now,' shrieked Jeannie, 'so don't go walking like a civilian. Ready?' Jeannie lifted his arm. 'Go!' His arm dropped and the music blared: *The first time I saw you I knew it was love.*

I didn't move. I didn't do anything. I wished I could be sick because then they would have to send me home. But I wasn't going to be sick. I was already empty. It felt like I was going to stand there forever, until the building fell down around my ears. Jeannie was coming towards me. He must have taken the high heels off because he moved like a man, an impossibly graceful man. He put his hand out and touched my shoulder. I couldn't breathe.

'Jennifer,' he said my name, quietly, gently, 'you've got everything, girl, you've got the looks, you've got the height – you've got the walk. You're going to walk beautifully. Let yourself do it.' I walked. My first attempt wasn't great but it wasn't laughably bad either. Jeannie, at ground level, walked alongside me shouting instructions that somehow made sense.

'That's it, that's it . . . keep your shoulders down, nice and relaxed. Lift your knees just a little higher . . . higher . . . not too much. Don't look at me, hon. Look straight ahead. Walk like you mean it. You've got to mean the walk!' My second attempt was better, more focused, more precise, but still a little stiff.

In my third walk all the pieces came together. It felt easy – it felt right; as though the air in front of me was rushing to get out of the way. The other girls were just a blur but I knew they were looking at me. And for the first time in my life I didn't mind being looked at. Jeannie was screaming, 'You got it, girl! You got it!'

As I reached the end of the catwalk, I saw Sophie jump to her feet and start clapping. The other girls looked at her like she was off her head, but I didn't care. All the rejections I'd had at castings and go-sees didn't seem so important now. I thought: I still have a chance at this. I can be a model.

7

My first photo-shoot was for *Clothes Crease in Hot Cars*, a trendy fashion magazine that ran for six issues. The editor wanted supermodel Francine Hope, for the cover of the launch issue. Madja said yes but insisted they use me as well. There was no casting. I turned up on the morning of the shoot, feeling like a fraud. All those lectures about how hard I would have to work to get anywhere and here I was – the unwanted part of a package deal.

No one in the *Clothes Crease* team seemed to mind that they had been forced to take me on, and looking back I can see why. Madja had given them Francine; if she'd asked them to take a gorilla as well they'd have stocked up on bananas.

'I hope you're not afraid of heights,' said Jack, the photographer. I looked down: the people on the pavement below were blurs of colour. I gulped. We were on the flat roof of an abandoned multistorey office building in north London. There were no protective railings to stop you if you got too close to the edge; I took a step back.

'No, I'm fine . . . heights . . . don't mind them, quite like them really . . .' Jack grinned. It was a nice, lopsided grin.

'That's the spirit. Now let's get started before this wind blows us off the bloody roof. Is Francine ready yet?'

'I sure am, honey,' said a sweet, low voice. I turned to see Francine Hope strolling on to the roof. She was tall, almost as tall as me, and, to my surprise, not really beautiful. I'd seen her in magazines and thought she was perfect – every single bit of her a ten out of ten. But in the flesh Francine looked like an alien. It was all so extreme: the tiny waist, the endless legs, the jutting cheekbones. She was a computer geek's idea of the perfect babe. Today the babe was dressed as a majorette, in a gold braided military jacket and tiny white skirt.

'Do ya all want me to twirl my little baton?' Without waiting for an answer she threw the gold stick high in the air, and caught it. The *Clothes Crease* team laughed and applauded. She ignored them, and walked straight over to me.

'You must be Jennifer Jones.' Francine was holding out her hand. I touched the end of her fingers by way of a handshake, and nodded, too tongue-tied to squeeze out a hello.

'Did your mama name you after the movie star, child?' She was in her early twenties but somehow she got away with calling me 'child'. I was so busy examining Francine's extraordinary face – all sharp lines and sloping planes – that it took me a few seconds to realise I had to her answer her.

'Er, I'm not sure, maybe . . .' I didn't want to admit I had no idea who Jennifer Jones was.

'Well I think she did. I just love those old movies. Jennifer Jones was just the most gorgeous girl. It suits you.' I blushed. The introductions over, Francine got down to business.

'Well, Jack honey, where do you want us?'

Jack wanted us at a picnic on the roof. It was an unmistakably American picnic: there were hot dogs and doughnuts, a huge cherry pie, strawberry milkshakes, fried chicken, bottles of Coke and Budweiser. It was all laid out on a red and white rug – a rug that, on closer inspection, turned out to be the American flag. Francine smoked patiently while the assistants put the finishing touches to the picnic.

We were wrapped in warm blankets while we waited although Francine, in a bum-skimming skirt, needed hers a lot more than I needed mine. I was dressed in a severe grey wool skirt suit. I looked like a librarian in a black and white film – you know, the type that turns out to be beautiful when the rich guy falls in love with her. Francine's look was just as weirdly old-fashioned – she belonged in a 1950s parade – but she was in full, blazing Technicolor. I didn't mind. She was the star of the show; I was an extra. It was fun just looking at her.

Jack's assistants couldn't get the chicken wings to behave. Jack wanted them piled high, but the chicken towers kept collapsing. After about fifteen minutes of building/collapse/ rebuilding Francine said, 'Jack honey, you know I have to be in New York tonight, don't ya? I don't wanna rush ya, baby, only time is passing . . .' Jack took the hint. He shooed the assistants out of the way, plucked a cherry from the pie and put it on top of a mound of wings.

'Ladies, your picnic awaits . . .'

'Come on, child, we're on.' Francine linked her arm through mine. We walked over to the picnic. Up close the food looked waxy and unreal. The cherry on the chicken was particularly gross. I hoped I wouldn't have to eat anything.

'Francine love, if you could lie down behind the chicken, on your side, with one hand supporting your chin . . .' Francine unhooked herself gently from my arm and did exactly as Jack asked.

'You gonna get me in trouble with my president, I'm sure this is disrespecting the flag.' Jack said no one would even be able to see the flag in the photos. Francine threw him a look. 'Sure they will – that's why it's there. You wanna be edgy – send up the old US of A; I get it. I can be edgy. Just don't try and pull the wool over my eyes, cos I ain't as dumb as I look.' Everyone became very quiet. Jack started to stammer, no of course he didn't think she was dumb, everyone knew she was smart . . . but Francine cut him off with a great hoot of laughter.

'Relax – I love your concept, Jack honey, it's so British. Now what d'you want Miss Jones to do?' Jack wanted me to cut up the cherry pie and then feed a slice to Francine. She didn't actually eat any of it – it turned out to be prop, made of plastic. But Francine acted eating the pie so well I kept having to check to see if she had actually taken a bite. The bottles of Budweiser, on the other hand, were real. Francine drank at least six of them in the next two hours. They didn't seem to have any effect on her.

Jack asked her to 'make it big' and she did – perfectly. Her poses had an exaggerated over-the-top quality: she didn't just lie down on the flag, she *acted* lying down on the flag. He kept screaming, 'Francine you're the best, the best, you are the BEST!' until Francine quipped, 'Honey, you sound just like my old high school professor,' and everyone laughed.

For the first half hour the plastic cherry pie gave a livelier performance than I did. Jack hardly seemed to notice I was there, and when he did it was only because I was doing something wrong.

'Head higher, Jen, arm further back, don't look at me, sweetheart, look at Francine, look at Francine.' I looked at Francine. And then I started to copy her. I tried to make everything I was doing 'big'. Francine was being the sexiest majorette ever; so I would be the stoniest-faced, never-been-kissed spinster librarian. I didn't just look at Francine, I glared – like she was a tramp and I was going to run her out of town. Francine spotted the change immediately.

'Oh baby, that's good – welcome to the show.'

Jack started telling me I was fabulous and fantastic and I started to believe him. It was intoxicating – a gorgeous guy, a guy who looked like he should be in a band, looking at me – and liking what he saw.

At one point he came over and stroked my face: 'Just tilt your head this way, that's it, that's it . . .' and my stomach lurched. Then he called over Susy, the make-up artist, and got her to smudge my lipstick with her thumb. 'I want her to look like the battle's over, like she can't withstand Francine's heat any more,' he told her. And Susy nodded her pretty blonde head and said, 'Sure, Jack, sure, that's so right.'

I only understood about a quarter of what was going on around me, but I could have gone on all day.

At about 4 p.m. Jack said the light was fading and suddenly the shoot was over.

Down on the street, all of us shivering against the cold, Francine kissed me on the cheek, and whispered in my ear: 'Madja told me you were something special, and she was right.' Then she slid into the back of a chauffeur-driven car and left for the airport. She was still wearing her harsh majorette make-up – and the little white skirt, over a pair of skinny jeans. The rest of stood in a huddle and watched the car disappear.

'I am completely happy,' said Jack. I felt pretty happy myself.

After a successful shoot you don't want the energy to drop. Performers – and good models are performers – find returning to the real world hard. It's the same for actors and musicians when they come off stage. There's a need to take the edge off reality – keep the buzz going. The last thing you want is to be on your own. Even if you've been working all day, and it's 1 a.m. and you're exhausted, being alone is just too much of a comedown. The people you've been working with are the only ones who get it; they know how high you're flying because they are too. This makes them your new best friends.

As I watched Francine's car disappear round the corner, I almost panicked: it was finished, I would have to go home now. When Jack said a mate of his lived nearby, and suggested we all go round and 'see what's hanging', I was so relieved I could have hugged him. But then I had an awful thought: maybe the 'we' in the invitation didn't include me. I mumbled something about needing to catch a train, but Jack said, 'Don't be stupid – you're with us, kid,' and sort of play-punched my arm. Susy said I had to come, and slipped her hand into mine; then Jack put his arm round my waist and the three of us set off down the street, with Petra, Jack's assistant, and two other guys and a girl trailing behind. I was beyond excited: the coolest people I'd ever set eyes on wanted me around.

As we set off down the street my phone buzzed in my jeans pocket. I knew it was a text from Stevie. I ignored it. Jack was talking to me about the shoot – how fantastic Francine was, what a great sport she'd been about the picnic in London in January concept – and I was nodding and saying, 'Yeah, she was great, amazing.' I thought I'd check my phone when we got to wherever we were going.

Jack's friend Zac, an artist of some sort, lived in a flat in a building that looked new and expensive. Jack banged on Zac's door for five minutes before getting a response.

'Hey, man,' said Zac, pulling the door open a few inches, 'I was sleeping.' He was bleary-eyed and his hair was sticking up at angles even product couldn't produce. And he was naked. I was so startled I heard myself make a kind of 'urrgh' choking noise. Then I was embarrassed at being embarrassed, because nobody else seemed to care. Susy stood up on her tiptoes and kissed him on the cheek. Petra looked his white, skinny body up and down and said, 'Working out again, eh Zac? You look *ripped.*' Naked Zac held the door open and we all trooped in. The flat was huge; there was nothing in it except the odd enormous piece of furniture and some small piles of rubbish. Jack hugged Zac.

'You got any vodka, man? We brought beer.' Zac nodded and padded off towards a vast, pale green fridge.

'Oh and put some clothes on, man – ladies present.' Zac swerved away from the fridge and picked up a pair of jeans from the floor. He didn't put them on straightaway, but ambled about, picking up random objects and setting them down again. Eventually, he came across a T-shirt, under a pizza box. He put the T-shirt on. And ate a slice of pizza. Only then, and agonisingly slowly, did he climb into his jeans.

Someone put some music on – female voices, singing in a language I didn't recognise, the volume loud. Susy began dancing on her own in the middle of the room. Zac lay down on the floor, next to a sofa that would have dwarfed a normal-sized room. The rest of us sat on the sofa and watched Susy. She had an odd dancing style – head thrown

back, eyes tight shut, arms waving limply above her head –
that made me feel quite queasy. Or it might have been
the beer. Jack had given everyone a bottle, and I drank
mine quickly. I didn't like the taste, but I wasn't about to
draw attention to myself by asking for a soft drink, and
besides, it gave me something to do with my hands. I
thought of Francine drowning bottle after bottle. I'd never
seen anyone drink so fast without being sick or, at the very
least, acting lairy.

Zac's place was really hot; if it was always this hot maybe
that was why he had seemed so comfortable naked. I wanted
to take my coat off but I was having doubts about the top I
was wearing, so I kept it on.

Jack left the sofa and lay down on the floor, next to Zac.
He pinched Zac's arm and said, 'Hey, hey,' until Zac opened
his eyes. Then they put their heads close together. When the
music stopped I heard Jack say, '. . . but that's Martha, man,
she can't help it, she doesn't get your art, she doesn't get you,
you know she doesn't, she was the same at school . . . You
and Martha, man, it's never going to happen.'

I looked around the flat; I couldn't see any paintings or
sculptures. There was nothing to suggest that an artist lived
here. Maybe Zac had a studio somewhere, filled with works
of genius. An image of Stevie hacking away at his clay horse
in art class popped into my head, and I pushed it away. I
wished I knew Jack as well as Zac did. Nobody was talking
to me. It was uncomfortable and a little bit boring. I didn't
know how to leave.

At last the sweltering heat forced me to my feet; I thought I might faint if I didn't get some air.

'You're not going, are you?' said Jack. It was enough to make me stay. I peeled off my coat and sat down on the floor. 'Where is that bloody vodka?' said Jack, complaining to no one in particular. 'Susy – you know where everything is – get us the vodka and some glasses, there's a good girl.'

Susy – who had been swaying in silence for the last five minutes – trotted off to the fridge. She came back with a bottle, and a tray filled with little glasses. Everybody sort of came to life. Even Zac sat upright long enough to drink several vodka shots.

Jack starting talking about the shoot again, telling everyone how great they'd been. He said the cover was going to be genius. He said *Clothes Crease in Hot Cars* was the most important new magazine since *The Face*. Everyone nodded and looked serious. I'd never even heard of *The Face* but his belief was infectious. I realised I was part of something important. I also realised that vodka was much better than beer; I was getting used to the burning sensation and it didn't really taste of anything. My tiny glass kept emptying and, magically, refilling.

At about midnight Zac – who was now mysteriously wide-awake – announced that we were all going to Martha's birthday party. He was quite insistent. It was Martha's birthday, and she was a great girl, and we had to go, because nobody should be on their own on their birthday, and she wanted him to be there, she was expecting him.

'Martha's birthday is in June, man,' said Jack, 'there's no party. You can't just turn up. She doesn't like it – seriously, Zac. She's talking about going to the police if you keep just showing up . . .' Zac just said over and over again that it was Martha's birthday and she wanted him there, Martha wanted him. He was on his feet and heading for the door.

Jack shouted after him; 'Have you got her a present?' Zac stopped, turned round and gazed at Jack. 'Because you know what a stickler she is. If you haven't got her a present, she'll be really disappointed. You can't just show up on her birthday without a present.'

Zac's face crumpled, and his whole body sagged . . . Jack rushed over, put his arms round his friend and held him up.

'We can go see Martha tomorrow, Zac, when we've got her a present. Tomorrow is better. Everything will be better tomorrow.'

'It's not really Martha's birthday, is it?' said Zac.

Jack shook his head and said no, it wasn't, and Zac started to cry.

It was at this point I stood up and said I thought I was going to be sick.

8

I woke up on a strange bathroom floor. I knew it was Zac's bathroom; I remembered being dragged there by Susy, straight after my think-I'm-going-to-be-sick announcement. No, I mean the floor was strange: it was covered in photographs.

When I managed to sit up a snapshot stuck to my cheek; I peeled it off and looked at it: a girl in a blue swimsuit and a white straw hat smiled out from the photo. She had her arm round two boys – Jack and Zac, looking younger and, in Zac's case, fatter and healthier. I looked around me. All the photos had a girl in them; I thought it was the same girl. Martha.

Someone, probably Susy, had put a towel over me. I shook it off, grabbed the side of the bath for support, and got to my feet. I wasn't sure if I had been sick but there was a vile taste in my mouth. The bathroom was freezing. I couldn't hear a sound from the rest of the flat. I thought: they've left me – they've left me alone in a flat with a crazy guy who carpets his floor with pictures of the girl he's stalking.

I was afraid that if I opened the door Zac would be standing there. I wasn't afraid of Zac, exactly, it was just that if I saw him I wouldn't know what to say. Thanks for letting me pass out in your bathroom? I'm sorry you're insane? I didn't have much experience of getting smashed and staying over at tortured artists' houses. I didn't have much experience of anything, except me and Stevie. I couldn't hide here all day, though. There was nothing else for it; I opened the door.

There was no sign of Zac. And I wasn't alone: Jack and Susy were asleep on the sofa. They looked comfortable in each other's arms, like it wasn't the first time. I hadn't realised they might be an item. It was – a surprise. My phone rang; it was still jammed inside my jeans pocket so the noise was muffled, but in the dead silence of the flat it was shockingly loud. I stepped back inside the bathroom, and closed the door.

'Hullo?' I croaked.

'Where the hell are you?' It was Stevie. 'Are you all right?' I mumbled something about staying over with some people from work.

'Are you hung over? You are, aren't you? You don't even drink!' I started to say something about a few vodkas, but Stevie cut me off.

'Forget that. Just get back here – I mean, like, *immediately*. Your mum thinks you stayed at mine last night, I had to cover for you. I'm not sure she believed me and if you don't show soon, she'll be round here, checking up, and then I will totally be in the shit because you've been out all night *having a good time with people from work!*' I didn't like his tone. He really spat those last words out. I thought he could have been more sympathetic. I felt awful. I sat on the edge of the bath, carefully.

'Oh and check your phone. I bet you've got like a hundred messages from Corinne. She even phoned me to try and find out where you were. I didn't bother lying to her. I said I had no bloody idea.' And then he hung up.

On the train going home, I found a window seat and pretended to sleep. At least I'd made it out of the flat without waking the sleeping pair. It was my only comfort. My head was banging and my mouth was dry as bone, and I wondered it it was possible to die from embarrassment. At the shoot I'd been a Focus model, working alongside Francine Hope. A few hours later I was stupid schoolgirl who couldn't hold her drink.

I wasn't ready to check my phone messages. I'd have to work up to it.

When I was a little kid and I got upset I'd make up stories in my head which made everything all right. Whatever upsetting thing had happened would happen in my story, only this time I would come out on top: the teacher who'd shouted at me would realise I was the most brilliant student she'd ever had. Quite often, I would die tragically, while performing a heroic act, and my mother and everyone who knew me would wear deepest black to my funeral and be sorry for ever.

After I started hanging out with Stevie I made up fewer and fewer stories. I didn't seem to need them so much. But now, without meaning to, I found myself in a love-triangle with Jack and Susy. In the story my character got the idea Jack and Susy were a couple but then found out it was all a funny misunderstanding, and they were really cousins or something. Jack told me he really liked me and wanted to go out with me. There was a sub-plot which had Zac murdering Martha and being sent to prison for life, and Jack being devastated, and me comforting him and the tragedy ultimately bringing us closer. I think there was a scene where we laid flowers on Martha's grave and then went to visit Zac in jail. It was all quite soothing.

But as the train pulled into the station, I knew I couldn't put real life off any longer, I pulled out my phone and checked my messages.

Corinne's weren't so bad. I was expecting a bollocking for failing to check in with her after the shoot, but she just wanted to let me know I had several castings coming up for London Fashion Week. For one horrible moment I thought I would have to go straight back to London. But no, I had some time to recover; the castings weren't for a couple of days. I phoned her, trying hard to sound normal and perky; maybe I overdid the perkiness, because she didn't buy it.

After she gave me detailed instructions about the castings, she said, 'So, you've been hanging out with the *Clothes Crease* crowd.' It wasn't a question.

'Well, yeah, after the shoot, you know . . .'

'Yes, I do know. I'm not your mother, Jen, I'm not going to tell you how to live your life. And, actually, socialising with photographers and clients is OK – people like to work with models they get on with. But you can't get wrecked before a big job. If the castings were today and you turned up looking the way you sound – rough – this would not be good. Do you get it?' I got it.

'Oh and by the way, I spoke to Jack.' For a lunatic moment I thought maybe he had phoned her to ask for my number. 'He said you did well. A lot of models just fade out next to Francine, but you held your own. If you can perform like that in the shows, we'll really be getting somewhere. Good work.'

I should have been delighted: my first job and I'd been a hit. But I felt a tiny stab of disappointment. Jack just liked me as a model. He probably was going out with Susy. I'd been kidding myself.

As I walked out of the station it occurred to me that Corinne also liked me as a model: as long as I did well at work she would be happy with me. If I had screwed up on the *Clothes Crease* shoot and then gone AWOL, she would have given me a much harder time. Corinne was lovely and smart and, most of the time, kind. But when it came down to it, for her, it was all about the work.

I had some grovelling to do before Stevie let it go.

'I'm not your secretary,' he whined, 'I shouldn't have to take calls from your mum and your agent. They both acted like it was my job to know your every movement and when I couldn't produce the goods they were pissed off – like I was lying, or something.

'Of course, I was lying to your mum – but I did it to be nice. I didn't want to worry her by telling her you had disappeared. But I think she knew I was lying and she sounded, I don't know, hurt or something. *You made me hurt your mum.*'

I said I was really, deeply sorry, I should have phoned her, I should have phoned him, I should have phoned Corinne. I was a rubbish friend, daughter and model. But could he please not shout because my head hurt?

I expected him to tell me I deserved to suffer, but he said, 'You do look awful,' and headed off to the bathroom. He came back with a glass of water and a couple of paracetamol. I gulped them down.

'I am sorry, Stevie, really.' I was sitting on his bed, his duvet wrapped around me.

'Yeah, well.' He lifted his hand and dropped it again, a gesture I knew meant so what, it's over, it's done. 'So tell me – what was it like?'

I told him: about Francine in her majorette outfit, and the fake picnic, and crazy Zac, and Susy dancing, and all the beers and vodka shots, and me waking up on the bathroom floor with Martha stuck to my face.

'From making pictures to waking up with them,' said Stevie, dreamily. 'God it's brilliant.'

But I didn't tell him about my stupid mini-crush on Jack,

even though he would have loved to hear all about it and would have been – now that he'd stopped being mad at me – sympathetic. I just didn't want to have the sort of conversation we always had when I had a fifteen-minute crush on some boy who didn't know I was alive. Stevie never told me who he fancied; we both had non-existent love lives but mine was the only one that was up for discussion.

For the first time in my life I didn't want him to know everything about me. Yesterday, at the shoot, I had been a working model; I had done something on my own.

When Stevie asked me if I thought I had a chance of getting booked for any of the London Fashion Week shows, I said no, probably not, it might be ages before I got another modelling job. But I was thinking of Francine saying, 'Welcome to the show,' when I started to perform properly at the shoot, and Corinne telling me, 'Jack said you did well . . .', and I was sure I would get booked for the shows. But there was no point telling Stevie that, it would just sound like I was full of myself. And besides, it really had nothing to do with him.

9

The last thing I felt before I stepped on to the runway was the seamstress's needle pricking my back; the zip had broken, I had to be sewn into the dress. I was trembling. I thought: Don't bleed, don't mark the dress. It was my first show at London Fashion Week – my first ever show. They say you always remember your first time. I still dream about mine.

'OK, Jen – go!' I step out. There's a wall of black at the end of the runway – the photographers, waiting for the best shot. I walk towards them; my legs seem to have a life of their own; I can't feel them, I'm floating, numb, high above them. There are people below me, on either side of the runway. I know who they are – fashion journalists, buyers, celebrities – but I don't see them, I feel them, the heat of their gaze burning into me.

There's a girl walking straight at me. She's too close, too close – we're both in the middle of the runway – I swerve and our sleeves brush together and it's OK, I walk on and suddenly I'm at the end. The cameras explode into life: I'm blind, I can't see anything, just intense white light. I pause, hold the position, count to two – show the clothes, show the clothes – turn and I'm off again, back down the runway.

Backstage the dressers are on me, ripping the stitches apart, pulling the dress off me. I stand with my arms folded over my breasts, naked in a flesh-coloured G-string. Someone is on the floor lifting one foot, and then the other, into high-heeled heavy shoes; it feels like I'm standing on my tiptoes in cement. I wobble. A voice – middle-aged, friendly – says, 'Can you walk in these shoes, lovie? Say no if you can't.' I say it's fine, I'll be fine, really.

I am fine – I'm walking. It's better this time, I don't have to swerve to miss the other girl, I just power past her, like she isn't there. When I make my turn the applause that has followed me all the way down the runway deepens, climaxes. I'm carried back on a wave of noise; it's not for me, I know it's not for me, it's for the clothes.

I hardly know what I'm wearing, but it's holding me tight and firm. I'm someone else in these clothes, someone who has never been afraid.

And then I'm shivering in my G-string, again, stepping out of the crazy high shoes and into light, strappy sandals and a long pink dress.

I'm about to step out – it's my final walk – when a man's voice says, 'Wait.' I turn: it's the designer, Martin Lawn, I recognise him from the casting. There's a blur of people all around him, but he's serious, serene. Another girl walks out, takes my place. What have I done wrong? Oh God, what have I done wrong? 'It's all right,' he says, 'you were great out there. I want you to close the show.' I stare at him, still too panicked to speak. He smiles. 'Don't look so worried, you get to wear the last dress. It's a promotion.' I nod. OK, OK.

And the hands are on me again, pulling off the pink dress. The new dress – the dress which will close the show – is the colour of nothing, the colour of skin; it slips over my body, a living thing.

The designer steps back, looks at me hard, takes it all in. 'No shoes – she needs to be barefoot.' I step out of the shoes before the dressers have time to move. I glance down and see folds of fabric covering my feet like a muddy puddle. 'The lips are too strong for the dress – blot the lips.' Someone places a tissue over my mouth, presses it, pulls away a layer of lipstick.

I walk out wearing nude lips and a nude-coloured dress. The fabric floats and clings, discovering my breasts, hips and arse, all the places in my body I usually keep hidden. People are on their feet, applauding. The nothing dress is a sensation and, because I'm wearing it, so am I.

It took less than a minute to change out of the dress and into my jeans and T-shirt. I looked like myself again – a gawky schoolgirl. But something had changed. On the runway I'd been beautiful and strong and mysterious. That girl – the girl on the runway – she couldn't just disappear now the show was over, could she? I needed to be her again.

'You did us proud, lovie.' It was the dresser – the one who

had checked if I could walk in the big shoes. She was folding the dress into a big protective bag. None of the other models said well done. Maybe some of them resented my success; I bet most of them didn't even notice it. They were dashing off to other shows. I had another show to go to too, but I couldn't move, not yet. I leaned against a wall and watched.

Half the audience seemed to have come backstage – they were kissing anything that moved. The biggest crowd was around the designer. I didn't expect him to speak to me, or even notice me, but he did. He came over, a trail of well-wishers behind him, and kissed me on the forehead.

'Thank you for making them see the dress.'

I didn't know what he meant but I didn't have time to answer because a TV crew dragged him away. And then a journalist stuck a tape recorder under my nose. My first media interview.

'Congratulations! You're new, aren't you? What's your name? How old are you? Where are you from?'

I don't know why it happened. I mean, they weren't exactly trick questions. I told her my name and age with no trouble at all. But then:

'Nowhere – I'm from Nowhere.' Stevie and mine's nickname for our town. Nobody else knew about it – we only ever said it to each other. And I had just announced it to a journalist.

Next morning I was pictured in the dress, on the front page of three national newspapers. Most of the coverage was about the designer; how with this collection Martin

Lawn must finally break through to the big time. (He did.) But I was definitely part of his story. One headline was all about me: *The girl from Nowhere steals the show*. The story that came with the picture quoted me calling my home town 'Nowhere'.

Stevie texted me at least thirty times. They all said much the same thing: OMIGOD FREAK – UR A FREAKIN STAR!!! YOU OWE IT ALL TO ME.

He kept up the texts for the next four days, until Fashion Week was over. I answered him during the few minutes when I was on my own – in the back of cabs, travelling between shows, or last thing at night, falling asleep in a hotel bed with the phone in my hand. Not once did Stevie suggest anything was wrong at school. He knew I was working. He didn't want me to worry.

10

When I arrived at the school gates, after dumping my suitcase at home, I was thinking about all the coursework I'd missed, and what a drag it would be to catch up. I had taken some schoolbooks with me to London and hadn't opened any of them. I guessed the teachers would give me more to take to Milan – the next stop in the fashion week circuit – and I wouldn't open those either.

I was early; the school grounds were almost deserted. One of the mobile classrooms had a big padlock on the door and the windows were boarded up; someone had trashed it, again. It seemed odd, suddenly, that I'd been coming here, almost every weekday, for five years. I had never even thought about it before. You don't, do you? School was – school: inevitable, like rain in winter or *Big Brother* in summer. I pulled my coat collar up and dipped my head against the wind. It was freezing.

'Hey, wait up!' I turned – Stevie. He had a bruise over his right cheekbone. Even apart from the bruise, he didn't look great.

'What happened to you?'

He shrugged. 'It's not as bad as it looks, don't make a big deal about it.' He glanced around, and put his hand on my elbow. 'C'mon, let's not hang about, we're going to be late.'

'No we're not, there's plenty of time – what are you doing?' Stevie was marching me down the corridor towards Mrs Blair's English class, at top speed.

'Didn't you get my text? I told you I'd pick you up at the station. You should have waited for me. Anything could have happened.'

I stopped dead in my tracks. The corridor was filling up. Someone bumped into me, didn't say sorry, walked on.

'What the hell are you talking about? What's going on?' He looked up at me; I was used to Stevie acting like a drama queen every chance he got but there was nervous look in his eyes I had never seen before.

'There's been some bother. Those pictures of you, in the newspapers, the Plastics brought them in and passed them around and now everybody knows. And some people aren't too happy.' I felt a swell of panic, it tasted bitter in my mouth. 'I'll fill you in later, but can we please get *inside.*'

Mrs Blair was alone in the classroom. She looked at me like she'd never seen me before.

'Jennifer, Stevie – why don't you two take seats at the front, where I can keep an eye on you. You've a bit of catching up to do, Jennifer. You've been away.'

Mrs Blair didn't stand for any trouble. Even the worst offenders in school more or less behaved themselves in her class. I think it must have been quite restful for them, having to sit quietly, a break from shooting their mouths off.

When Karen Reilly (one of the leading Skanks) walked in and said, 'Oh, look who it is – the big "supermodel",' Mrs Blair didn't even look up. 'That's enough from you, Karen. Take your seat and be quiet. I don't want to hear another word.' The class was quiet, quieter than usual, for the next ten minutes or so.

The whispers started as soon as Mrs Blair turned her back on us, to write on the whiteboard. Something soft hit the back of my head and fell to the floor. There were giggles. I thought I knew what it was but I picked it up anyway: a ball of scrunched up newspaper – my front page picture. *The girl from Nowhere steals the show.* 'Ugly Bitch', in red biro, was scrawled across my face.

'I'll take that, Jennifer,' said Mrs Blair. She took the paper from my hand, looked at it briefly, and threw it in the bin. 'I'm not going to bother asking who did that. If anything like it happens again I will hold the entire class responsible. Spiteful and jealous behaviour is bullying. And bullying is not tolerated in this school.'

This was true, as far as it went. Bullies who beat up their victims on a regular basis got excluded. Major acts of violence were not tolerated. But spite, jealousy and all-round nastiness? It wasn't 'behaviour' you could control; it was just how people were.

In the corridor, on our way to our next class, we had company. I thought for a second about Martin Lawn being mobbed after his show. Of course, this mob didn't want to kiss us.

Leanne Cooper started things off by asking me if I thought I was something special. There is no right answer to this kind of question, so I kept quiet. Soon there were so many comments flying around I couldn't have picked out one to answer, even if I had wanted to; it was just a buzz of hate-filled noise. Stevie stuck close to my side but said nothing. By the time we reached the classroom I was finding it hard to breathe. No one touched me; not even a shove or a push.

When the bell went we didn't have to face any corridor action because our next class was in the same room. I stared straight ahead, willing the teacher to be on time, as the new arrivals filed in.

Julie Smith, a Plastic I'd never had anything to do with before, sat next me and whispered, 'So, how was it? Being a model, I mean. Was it really exciting? That dress you wore was amazing.' I looked at her. She meant it. She was interested – impressed. I tried to smile, muttered something about it being really good, you know, and then the teacher walked in and the lesson began.

We decided not to risk the school canteen at lunchtime. There was a café in town, a ten-minute walk away, where nobody from school ever went; its customers were old ladies and mums with buggies. Stevie and me went there sometimes when we couldn't face school, and this was one of those times. We never made it.

In the playground, they were waiting for us. I'd never seen the Skanks and the Plastics so comfortable together. There were more of the Skanks and they were nastier, obviously, but the digs from the Plastics hit me harder. The Plastics were genuinely surprised that someone who looked like me could be a model.

We tried to keep walking, but the circle surrounding us got tighter and tighter until we had to stop and let whatever was going to happen, happen. Someone said I 'deserved a kicking for dissing the town' and calling it 'nowhere'. Paula Tweedy said I was an 'ugly minging bitch' and if anyone rearranged my face it could only be an improvement. A Plastic said, to no one in particular, 'I mean she's not good-looking. How can she be a model? She doesn't even look like a girl.' Someone said, 'Yeah, total weirdo – look at the dwarf gay boy she hangs out with.' All of these comments were from girls.

When Dwayne Smith arrived, the circle parted to let him in. Everybody quieted down. Dwayne pushed one hand through his hair, coughed a little to clear his throat, made them wait for it: 'You a model? Well, are you?' I nodded, yes. Yes. 'Christ almighty.' He shook his head in disbelief. 'You may be a model, love, but I bet you die a virgin.' The girls roared. I closed my eyes.

'That's not very nice, Dwayne,' said a soft, clear voice from the back of the crowd. I looked over the rows of heads; it was Clare, with Louise. They moved forward, weaving their way around the other girls with a string of small courtesies: excuse us, sorry, please, thank you.

Maybe Dwayne was sorry he'd just behaved like a pig in front of two girls he fancied. Or maybe he'd used up his one brain cell on the 'virgin' crack, and was all out of conversation. Either way, we didn't hear anything else from Dwayne.

'Hi, Jen, hi, Stevie,' said Louise. We said 'hi' back. 'We haven't seen you for a while. C'mon.' Louise hooked her arm into mine; Clare did the same with Stevie. 'Let's get a sandwich.' The two tiny blondes walked us through the crowd. There were protests – the odd 'Where are you going with those freaks?' kind of thing. But the twins just ignored the remarks.

The four of us walked clear of the school, checked we weren't being followed, and stopped at a bus shelter. I sat down on the bright plastic bench. I was exhausted and, suddenly, hungry.

'Thanks,' said Stevie, 'thanks for that. It was getting rough back there. I thought we were for it.'

'That's all right.' I didn't know which twin was speaking, I was staring at the ground. 'After what happened to you, we thought we'd better keep an eye out.' I looked up. Clare was standing really close to Stevie. She was gazing at him with a really soppy expression on her face – like he was an injured puppy or something.

'What happened to Stevie?' I asked.

The twins looked at each other. 'You don't know?'

'It was nothing,' said Stevie. 'I got hit.' His hand drifted up to the bruise on his face.

'Over me? Someone hit you because of me?' I'd assumed it was his dad who had caused the bruise; he could be pretty free with his hands.

'Yeah well, they were saying stuff . . .' He didn't tell me any more about it. He wouldn't even tell me who had hit him. 'You don't need to know, you've got to forget about all of this, not let it get to you. It'll die down, it will. Those idiots – they'll be making someone else's life a misery next week. You and the modelling thing – they'll get used to it.' He tried to smile, moved closer to me and rubbed my arm; I thought of Corinne. Clare and Louise murmured yes, yes, Stevie's right, it'll be OK.

I stood up, dug a tissue out of my pocket and blew my nose. I remembered there was a bottle of water in my bag; I fished it out and took a swig. I felt calmer. Everything I'd been dreading, right from the start, had just happened. School had found out about the modelling; the shit storm I had been expecting had rained down. I'd been mocked and hated. It was a relief. I felt, oddly, almost happy.

'I don't care if they get used to me being a model. I'm not going back to school. I'm leaving.'

There was a long silence. I think Stevie knew I was serious, that I had made my mind up. When he said, 'But what about your A levels?' it was because he couldn't think of anything else to say.

'The London shows went really well for me. I can do this full-time. I don't need A levels to be a model. In my position, exams are just a waste of time.' A hundred times or more,

Stevie had said to me that exams created wage slaves – the best jobs, the ones really worth having, just needed raw talent. But he didn't agree with me now. He just stood there, watching the traffic pass by.

'We better be going, leave you to it.' It was Clare who spoke. The twins left the shelter, started to head back to school. They had only gone a few paces when they paused and looked round at us.

'Bye, Jen – and good luck with the modelling,' said Clare.

'We think it's brilliant,' said Louise.

I waited until they were out of sight. 'So, shall we get some lunch, then? What do you fancy?'

'I've got to get back. Lunch hour is over.'

'Bunk off,' I said. I couldn't stop myself. 'Let's celebrate my big decision. Today must be worth one of your sick notes. *I'm leaving school.*' Stevie turned to face me; he looked pale, worn out, and utterly miserable.

'You're not just leaving school, you're leaving me, and you don't even realise it. You don't even care.'

'Of course I care – don't be stupid.' This didn't come out the way I meant it to: it sounded snappy, irritated. 'So I'm moving to London. So what? We'll still be mates. I'll keep in touch, you can come and stay with me at weekends in London, it'll be great, really it will. Nothing is going to change – nothing.'

Stevie just shook his head. As he started to walk away I could see tears in his eyes. I thought: how dare you. All the years we'd spent dreaming of escaping this dump of a town, and now I was doing it and he was making me feel bad.

I shouted after him: 'You're a bloody hypocrite, Stevie! You're the same as the rest of them. Do you hear me? You're jealous! You're just jealous!'

But Stevie kept walking.

11

I didn't tell Corinne about the angry mob, chasing me off the school premises with pitchforks and burning crosses. I made leaving school sound like a well thought out decision, made in a calm frame of mind. The whole name-calling and bullying scene was just too much drama. And besides, the things they had said . . . I felt ashamed – I didn't want her to know.

Corinne was pleased. She didn't come straight out and say, 'You've abandoned your education, hurrah! No need to wait until you're eighteen after all,' but I could hear the relief in her voice. I guess it made things simpler for her. From now on I would be available 24/7.

'The London shows were really good for you, Jen – I can't remember the last time a new girl made such a big impression. Right now, you're hot. We need to take advantage of that. Now you don't have to fit work round school we can say "yes" to every decent client who comes along.'

I leaned back against a pillow and stared up at Tobey Maguire; he was looking a bit dog-eared. He'd been there a long time. Maybe I was getting too old to have posters of film stars on my bedroom walls. It was strange, sitting on my bed, looking at Tobey, while talking to my agent about 'clients'.

'Everyone who is anyone will be at Milan. Do well there and we're talking serious money.'

I don't like talking about money, it's boring and kind of embarrassing. I leave all that stuff to my accountants and financial advisers. But at least now I know the basics: I know how much I'm worth. Back then I was a complete baby – clients could have paid me in sweeties and I would have waved my little rattle and gurgled, happily. But when it came to business, Corrine expected all her girls to behave like adults. I had to make an effort.

'Serious money? Fantastic. Do designers in Italy pay a lot for models to appear at their shows . . . or, what?'

'Well, it's not like the early nineties of course . . . hang on a minute.' I heard a rustling sound and a soft thump. 'What a relief to get those shoes off, and people say wedges are comfortable . . . Yes, in the nineties the top girls could get twenty thousand pounds for a three-minute walk in Milan. But it's still respectable. The London shows were pocket money really – just a couple of hundred a show. But you should pick quite up a few grand in Milan.'

I sat bolt upright. 'As in – thousands of pounds?'

Corinne laughed. 'Yes, Jen. Thousands of pounds.'

I looked at Tobey. He looked back at me, with, I thought, new interest.

'Of course your earnings from the shows will be nothing

compared to what you could make from advertising campaigns. That's where the real money is. The shows are just – window-dressing. They get you seen by potential clients. That's what it is all about.'

Stevie would have loved this conversation; he always wanted us to be rich. But we hadn't spoken since I walked out of school, yesterday. Which meant I had nobody to tell.

'Are you there, Jen? Jen?'

'Oh yeah, sorry, I lost you for a minute, but I'm back now.' I heard a mobile phone ringing.

'Look, I better get that . . . Are you clear about the arrangements for Milan?' said Corinne.

'Meet Sophie at the check-in desk at the airport, 6.30 a.m.' We'd been through this about three times already.

'And don't forget your passport. Good. Enjoy. Work hard. And keep an eye on little Sophie, she can be a bit – you know. I'll see you when you get back.' The line went dead.

I held the mobile in my hand and stared at it. I wanted to call Stevie – sort of. I thought about what I would say to him – nothing about how minted I was going to be, that was for sure. It would probably not be a good idea to go on about Milan either. He would be bound to make some quip about me living it up in Planet Fashion. And I couldn't tell him I was actually a bit nervous about leaving school and modelling full-time because he would be all over that like a rash. So what could I talk to him about? What was left? Nothing.

He was the one who had walked off. Maybe it was up to

him to make the first move. And besides, I didn't have the time for any more kid's stuff. I had a plane to catch tomorrow. I had to go to work.

I leaned over the edge of the bed, and dragged my hand through the open suitcase. It was full of dirty clothes, from my week in London. Later, I thought, I'll sort it out later. I've got plenty of time.

'Keep your hair on, love,' said the driver. 'We're here now.' I fell out of the cab. As I sprinted into the terminal building, my wheelie case bouncing along behind me, I didn't feel like a Focus model on her way to the shows in Milan. I felt like a kid who shouldn't be allowed to cross the road on her own. All the confidence I'd built up during London Fashion Week seemed to be draining out of my Shelleys boots.

Sophie phoned me at 7 a.m.; I had been running round in circles for fifteen minutes. I started to say some gibberish about running late and having to dry my underwear with a hairdryer and everything in my suitcase being damp. Sophie stayed calm: 'It's OK, Jen. Tell me where you are. I'm coming to get you.' When I saw her face in the crowd, I could have cried with relief.

A small plump woman with thick dark hair and olive skin was holding a sign that said 'Focus – Sophie Lamb & Jennifer Jones'. Sophie shook the woman's hand and said something – in rapid Italian.

The woman shook her head. 'No, dear, I'm from the

London office; they sent me over for Fashion Week, it's all hands on decks. You two look big enough to look after yourselves but there's a couple of babies back at the apartment. We better get back sharpish or they'll be crying for their mothers. The name's Maria.'

An hour later we were in Milan. I peered out from Mama's tiny car through a side window as small as a porthole: Milan was a lot like London – the same big city mix of cars and people and shops.

I had been to Spain with my mum on a couple of package holidays in hotel resorts, but this was my first time abroad in a real city with people going about their daily business. I wondered if Sophie had been here before; she hadn't said anything on the plane, but then, she hadn't mentioned speaking Italian either. I glanced at her; she looked fresh, uncrumpled. I was pretty sure the clothes in her pink case were dry and ironed.

'I didn't know you spoke Italian, Sophie.'

'A little. Not as well as Spanish or French, but I can get by. I worked in Italy, quite a lot, when I was younger. You pick it up. Oh look!' She pointed out of the window. 'I used to go to that little bakery with my parents when I was kid. My brother was just a baby then. It's still there, how lovely.'

Look after little Sophie, Corinne had said. Right. If anybody was going to need looking after, it was me. I had calmed down a lot on the plane but now I was afraid, all over again: afraid that a friend was cleverer than me and had been to more places and knew more stuff. I was going to spend Milan Fashion Week trailing along behind Sophie while she spoke Italian and bought bloody pastries from her favourite bakery.

Sophie squeezed my hand.

'It's all a bit much, when you first arrive, isn't it? I always feel – lost. Don't you?' And I squeezed her hand back and said, yes, I felt just like that.

The apartment was small, modern and clean. I didn't know what an Italian apartment was supposed to look like. I suppose I thought there might be a balcony. There wasn't. Maria showed us round; she explained how everything worked in minute detail – even how to turn the taps in the bathroom off and on, although they were perfectly ordinary taps. When she was demonstrating what to do with the shower curtain – 'inside the bath, like this, to keep the water in' – I started to giggle. Sophie nudged me in the ribs and I nudged her back; soon we were both sniggering like a couple of schoolgirls. Maria didn't seem to mind.

'Oh you can laugh, but you wouldn't believe the daft things some of you girls get up to. The agency had a lovely place in Paris, all the top girls fought to stay there. A Latvian girl managed to blow it up. Said she'd never cooked with gas before.'

I said we'd be very careful.

'Make sure you are – and look after yourselves too. My mum's from Milan but I've never been keen, there are too many . . . Oh there you are!'

We turned and saw two girls standing in the bathroom doorway. They must have crept in as softly as cats. They were strikingly similar – both had long brown hair, parted in the middle, narrow, straight bodies and round pale faces. They were dressed identically in skinny jeans, short jackets and flat, fringed boots. They looked about twelve.

'We went out,' said one of the girls, 'for milk.'

'And biscuits,' said the other one. 'We got biscuits as well as milk.'

'Well done, girls,' said Maria. 'Now do you think you could put the kettle on? These young ladies – this is Jen and this here is Sophie – have been travelling all morning, they must be parched.' The girls padded off towards the kitchen.

'Er, Maria – what are their names?' said Sophie.

'Oh Lord, I forgot! They're both called Nadia. Quite handy, that. To tell the truth, I have trouble telling them apart. There's another girl supposed to be staying here, Arabella, but I doubt if you'll be seeing much of her. Her father moved her into a hotel. Apparently this place isn't up to her usual standards.'

Maria said she had some other model apartments to check up on, but she'd back by 11 p.m. to make sure we were all tucked up in bed.

'This will probably be your only night off – it'll be work, work, work from tomorrow – so you might as well go out and see the sights. Not that there's much to see in Milan. I don't know why the Italians can't hold their fashion week in Rome or Venice, I really don't. But try and enjoy yourselves.' She headed off down the corridor, stopped, swore softly, and scuttled back.

'Just one more thing, girls – don't drink, take drugs or get pregnant. Not on my watch.'

As soon as Maria was gone, I burst out laughing. Sophie said, 'Oh don't, she means well, and she's lovely, really,' but she was giggling too. The Nadias just stared blankly at us; I wondered if they were so innocent that Maria's sex 'n' drugs warning had gone over their heads. I wanted to ditch them for the night but Sophie said it wouldn't be fair. We were stuck with them.

The Nadias spent the afternoon trying on each other's clothes and experimenting with various shades of neon eyeshadow and gloopy lip-gloss. Sophie didn't wear make-up when she wasn't working and my routine – matt red lips and nothing else – took two minutes, so we had a lot of time to kill. We watched soaps on TV. Every half hour or so the Nadias emerged from their room and paraded their latest look, blocking our view of the TV. It was annoying. The Nadias' outfits all looked the same but their make-up got steadily brighter and shinier.

Sophie flicked TV channels, pausing at a programme about Milan Fashion Week. I'd almost forgotten, for the last few hours, why we were here. There was a clip of Francine Hope striding down the runway at last season's Versace show. I could hardly believe I had worked with her. She looked so good it was inhuman. There must have been forty or fifty models walking behind her; the effect was slightly frightening: a model army on the march. I hadn't seen anything like it at the London shows.

'This is making me nervous,' I said, 'doesn't it make you feel nervous?'

Sophie shrugged and said, so softly I could hardly hear her, 'It makes me feel tired, just – tired.' She got up and walked quickly to the Nadias' room. 'Girls, you both look great. We're going out.'

The centre of Milan was a fifteen-minute walk from our apartment. Sophie led the way. I was impressed but she said it was easy; all we had to do was follow the signs to the Piazza del Duomo.

When we got there, after walking through streets of ordinary shops and offices, I thought: so this is what Italy looks like. The piazza was an elegant square dominated by the Duomo, an eye-poppingly ornate cathedral.

'It's pretty, isn't it?' said Sophie.

'The square is, sure, but the church? I'm not keen. It reminds me of the cake my Aunt Pat always bakes on special occasions – too much icing.' I expected Sophie to laugh but she just looked at me.

'You're so clever, Jen. I would never come up with something like that, I would never even think it.'

Groups of people our age were hanging about on the steps of the cathedral. Or maybe they were twenty-five-year-olds with nowhere to go. They were young but too well dressed, too glossy to be teenagers. Suddenly I wished I had made a bit more effort. Maybe the Nadias had had the right idea. I glanced at them: they looked as if they had been dipped in glue and rolled in pink glitter. On second thoughts, that wasn't the right way to go either.

We chose a café at random and sat down at an outside table. Milan in February is damply cold but the dozens of outside tables were filled with people.

'Look at all the women in fur coats,' I whispered to Sophie. 'Omigod – there's an old bloke over there wearing one too. Look!'

'I know, it's horrible,' said Sophie, and she gave a little shudder. 'So cruel.' I hadn't really been thinking about the minks and foxes that had given their skins for fashion. I'd just been struck by the oddness of it all. These people were so dressed up – and so grown up. Maybe it was because I'd gotten used to the London fashion scene – all the thirty-year-olds who dress like eighteen-year-olds – but in Milan everybody looked forty.

I whispered to Sophie: 'They all look so old.'

She giggled, like I'd said something terribly rude. 'I know – but think how we must look to them.' In need of a makeover, probably. Sophie was lovely in her printed dress and thick woolly tights and I was no more hideous than usual in a 1960s minidress (worn over black jeans) that I'd picked up in a Save the Children Shop in Hoxton. I was actually quite chuffed with my purple suede pixie boots. But I could just imagine an Italian stylist forcing us both into tailored separates and beige. We were fine for London but the London look didn't cut it in Milan.

We were all gazing at our menus when a clear, crisp voice said, 'Oh hello.' I looked up. It was a pale girl with red bobbed hair; she was with a tall gangly man with greying red hair.

'Daddy, this is Nadia and Nadia, my flatmates for all of fifteen minutes.' The Nadias smiled weakly. 'And you must be Jennifer and Sophie. I was quite happy to stay in the apartment with you girls, you know, but Daddy declared it a dump and now I'm stuck in his palace of a hotel, pining for someone to talk to.'

'Monstrous girl,' said 'Daddy', looking not in the least embarrassed. 'I'm sure I never said "dump". I don't know why she let the agency put her in a flat, there was no need. Have you young ladies eaten yet? Let me take you out to dinner. You would be doing me a great favour. It's the least I can do, after depriving Bella of your company.' I was too taken aback to say anything, but Sophie squeaked out something along the lines of no thank you, we couldn't possibly.

'Nonsense. I insist.' And that was that.

Bella's father paid our drinks bill and Sophie and I got up to go.

The Nadias didn't budge. 'We have plans.' Sophie and I stared at them, amazed. 'Oh – they're early.' And with that the girls got up and strolled over to two boys on scooters, in the middle of the piazza. Then they kissed the boys, hopped on the back of the bikes, and sped off.

'Do you think they'll be all right?' said Sophie. She sounded horrified.

Bella slipped her arm through Sophie's. 'Of course they will. You didn't buy that "butter wouldn't melt" routine, did you? They're as tough as old boots, those two. I knew it as soon as I laid eyes on them. Come on – let's eat.'

12

In London Fashion Week a lot of designers do everything on a shoestring, and it shows. I would turn up for a casting at the address the agency had given me and think, this can't be right. Instead of the minimalist studio I had been expecting, there would be a damp hole of a place, cluttered with half-finished clothes, leftover junk food, and the designer's hanger-on mates from fashion college. I'd shivered a lot because some of the designers couldn't afford heating; one didn't have a toilet (you had to nip round the corner to the pub). Milan did things differently.

My first casting, at 7 a.m., was held in an eighteenth-century ballroom. I walked under chandeliers, past huge gilt mirrors and portraits of women in dresses so extravagant they could have been designed by John Galliano. The only non-exquisite thing in the vast room was the designer himself – he looked like a hobbit in sunglasses. He didn't say a word to me, just stared straight ahead, while a woman with short white hair whispered in his ear.

At that first casting I was so overwhelmed by the venue, I forgot to be nervous. What did it matter if I was auditioning for a part in Milan Fashion Week? I hardly knew what century I was in.

Sophie knew exactly where she was. When she came back into the reception area I took one look at her face and asked if it had really been that bad.

'No – at least they didn't say anything nasty, but they didn't have to. You can always tell. They look at you and then their eyes sort of . . . slide off.'

Our second appointment was at a big name fashion label's headquarters; I'd never realised an office – and the colour beige – could be so beautiful. The casting went better for Sophie. I noticed that a lot of the other girls there had her 'look' – the same soft prettiness.

I knew they wouldn't want me – I didn't know they would be so obvious about it. I didn't even get to finish my walk. I'd taken about five steps when the designer screeched, 'Stop!' It was as if he couldn't bear me to get any closer; he actually covered his eyes with his hand. I was so embarrassed, I froze. An assistant appeared out of nowhere and led me to the side of the room. This was witnessed by about forty other girls. The next girl up did even worse.

As she paused to do her turn, the designer barked, 'How heavy are you?' She told him. 'Liar. You are at least two kilos heavier. You girls eat like pigs and then you come here and think we won't notice. Can you lose two kilos before my show? No, I didn't think so. Next!'

Casting numbers three and four were fast, efficient and polite.

Number five was excruciating. The designer and his stylist kept up a running commentary on the girls'. The comments I remember include:

'Is she Asian? She looks Asian to me. I told the agency, no ethnics this year, we're not doing ethic.'
      'Why is she walking like that? Is she trying to be funny? Tell her she's not funny. She's a mess.'

'Ugh! Look at her tits! I cannot have tits in my dresses.'

At our sixth casting we ran into Bella. I asked her where she had been all morning.

'Oh, this is my first casting. I told my booker, "Don't make any appointments for me before 11 a.m., I'm no good in the morning." ' I stared. Bella shrugged. 'You can't let the agency boss you around. They're working for us, remember.'

It was news to me.

'Bella's right,' said Sophie, when I asked her about it, later. We were in a cab, on our way to our first fitting. 'The models are the talent – we employ the agency to represent us. Which means, if you think about it, that we're Corinne's boss. And Madja's. Only it never feels like that, does it? I've had an agent since I was five years old and I've always done exactly what I've been told. When my little brother was sick last year I wanted to be there when mum brought him home from hospital, but my agent at the time booked me for a cereal commercial in Germany. I didn't see Ben for a month. Focus are a lot nicer . . . ' she looked out of the car window, 'it's easier than it was.'

I was booked for thirty shows in Milan. Sophie got booked for fifteen. Every designer who got to see Bella wanted her; she accepted about a third of the bookings she was offered.

'Well, it's not physically possible to do more than five shows a day.' She twisted some linguine around her fork. It was 9 p.m.; we were having dinner together at Bella's hotel before going back to work. I had a fitting at 11 p.m.; Sophie had one at midnight. Bella was going to an after-show party.

'I'm doing seven shows on Thursday,' said Sophie, quietly.

'I'm doing nine,' I added. Bella put her fork down.

'Oh you poor things. That is *horrible*.' Then she picked up her fork, reloaded it with food, and carried on eating, quite cheerfully. A waiter topped up Bella's glass with mineral water and drifted away. Sophie and I had barely touched our drinks but if our glasses had been empty I doubt if he would have noticed. Bella hoovered up attention until there was none left over for anyone else. I hadn't noticed it on our first evening together, because her father was with us and he attracted even more attention than Bella.

Waiters approached Bella's father as if they were not just happy to serve him but honoured. They actually bowed. I couldn't work it out. I'd always thought that only rich and famous people brought out the flunkey in strangers, but I'd never heard of Bella or her father and they didn't exactly look minted. Bella's wardrobe was jeans and jumpers in winter and (I later discovered) jeans and T-shirts in summer. Her father wore a coat with a button missing and his hair was wild and straggly and in need of a cut. No one would have mistaken him for an Italian.

And yet I knew they must have money to be able to afford this hotel – Bella had hardly been exaggerating when she called it a palace. I found out later, that's exactly what it was, two centuries before it became a hotel.

I looked around me: the restaurant was like a scene from *Poirot* on ITV1 on a Sunday night; the heavily made-up woman and her bored-looking daughter at the next table – they could have been a murderous duchess and a young heiress. I was tired after a long day, my mind was starting to drift, I had to go back to work after dinner . . .

'Ice cream? Would you like some ice cream?' Bella's clear voice was like a splash of cold water. 'I know it's freezing February but I think it's a pity to stay in Milan and not have the ice cream. It's rather good.' We had the ice cream. Bella was right – I'd never tasted ice cream like it before. This was definitely a step up from McDonald's with Stevie. I couldn't relax though, I wasn't used to eating out, not like this, in a proper restaurant where the waiters moved so smoothly they seemed to float across the floor. The waiters, the room, the food – they made me feel I had to sit up straight. It was almost irritating how relaxed Bella was. She could have been eating a bowl of cereal in her pyjamas, in front of the telly.

I couldn't tell how Sophie was feeling, or if she was feeling anything in particular. She looked fine, but she hadn't said much all evening. In the piazza, on our first night, Sophie had ordered drinks at the café, in Italian, and explained what all the local dishes were on the menu. But here she had left all of that up to Bella, even though Bella didn't seem to speak a word of Italian. The Sophie I had just been getting to know – the Sophie who knew what to say and what to do – had been quietly hidden away again, because she wasn't needed.

Sophie didn't say anything memorable that evening, except this:

'Why did you become a model, Bella? Only, if you don't mind me saying, you don't seem very . . . keen.' I thought: that's just what I want to know.

Bella leaned back in her chair and yawned; the chair teetered backwards. A waiter passing by put his hand out and steadied her.

'Oh I don't give a stuff about modelling, I mean why would I – why would anyone? Daddy's quite right – it is just prancing up and down wearing stupid clothes made by a bunch of old queens. But it is stupidly well paid and it's better than being at school. I've never got on with school. In fact my last school asked me to leave, so I thought I might as well bugger off and do the modelling thing for a year or two.' I was amazed. Until that moment I had assumed that Bella must have tried harder than she let on to be so successful as a model – I thought she had to care, even if she was too proud to let anyone know. But it wasn't an act. Bella wasn't faking casual about modelling – she *was* casual. It had all come easily to her and she didn't give a damn. I felt like a drudge next to her, a model school swot.

Being this close to Bella's self-confidence made me feel quite strange, almost queasy – it was like staring over the edge of a bottomless well.

There was a scraping noise – Sophie pushing her chair back. 'I'm going to the loo,' and she took off across the crowded restaurant, weaving, a little uncertainly, between the tables. I wondered if she was upset about something, if I should go after her.

'You're very fond of Sophie, aren't you?' said Bella.

'I suppose so. I haven't known her very long.'

'But you look out for each other, I can tell, you're quite a team. It's nice. She's a sweet little thing, isn't she?'

I didn't like Bella talking about Sophie as though she were a child or a pet, the moment her back was turned. So I said, 'Sophie's very clever actually. She can speak fluent Italian – and Spanish, and French. And she can find her way all over Milan without a guidebook. And she has years of experience as a model – years and years.' And as soon as I had said all this I realised that I was the one who sounded like a child. A child sticking up for her new best friend. I might hit Bella with my toy in a minute. I was an embarrassment.

'There – that's what I mean: you two are a team, you look out for each other. I think it's great. I've met hundreds of people since I started modelling a year ago but none of them are my friends, not really. I expect when I leave the business no one will care, or even notice I have gone. And I won't miss them a bit.'

I didn't have time to say anything because Sophie came back to the table and managed to knock over a glass as she sat down. I started to mop up the spillage with a huge stiff napkin but then one of the gliding waiters appeared and took over. Sophie and I sat like naughty children while Bella ordered coffees. I said I didn't drink coffee, but Bella said we needed them to stay awake.

When the waiter was gone, she asked us where our fittings were, and which designers we were working for. It was first time she had shown any interest in our work.

'Well it all sounds very – professional. Sometimes I wish I had more of a work ethic. My mother says if I had been born in LA I would be a size zero airhead, falling out of limousines with no knickers on.' I could think of nothing to say to this. Sophie took a small bite out of the tiny biscuit that came with her coffee. It was getting late, I needed to go, but Bella said, 'Wait, just a second.'

She called a waiter over and asked if she could have a pen; he came back with a fountain pen. She scribbled something on her linen napkin and pushed it across the table. I glanced down – it was spattered with ink blots – and read, 'To Jen and Sophie, please come . . .'

'It's an invitation to my eighteenth birthday party . . . it's ages away but I wanted to let you know now. I'll be texting everyone of course, but an invitation on linen is impossible to turn down, don't you think? It's practically a royal command.'

'Won't they mind,' I said, 'I mean . . . the hotel, if we take this away? Isn't it stealing?'

Bella laughed. 'Oh Jen, you are wonderful. So serious. My mother would love you. They won't mind at all. Don't you know? My father owns the hotel.'

13

Sophie, Bella and I looked so different we were rarely cast
for the same shows. Designers don't want the best girls or the
most beautiful girls – they want the girls who fit the look
they're selling. So you get classic blondes following each
other down the runway, or tomboys with short hair, or pretty
brunettes with fake tattoos on their shoulders. What you
almost never get is a show where different girls are mixed up
together. When all the models in a show look the same the
audience don't really see them at all – they see the clothes.
Which is the point.

At a casting the dress tries on the girl; if the girl doesn't
fit she gets put back on the rail. This is particularly true of
Milan. In my first season in Milan a designer dropped me a
day before his show, at the fitting, because a dress came up
short on me. It was easier to get another girl than to let the
hem down an inch.

Some designers hardly change their look from season
to season. Mr Armani (who is lovely to work with, by the
way, a real gentleman) won't choose a girl just because she
is 'hot', she has to suit his clothes – which are always

beautiful, always elegant. But some designers trade on novelty and surprise; the press turn up at the shows thinking, 'What will he do this time? What trick will he pull out of the box?'

In Milan there aren't many tricks; designers who show in Milan don't experiment, the way they do in London, or imagine they are creating art, which some do in Paris. They are making clothes which will sell. Maybe that's why we were such a sensation when Giovanni sent us down the runway together. A tall boyish girl with short black hair, a soft blonde, a haughty redhead – we must have looked so peculiar walking in a row, arms linked.

Giovanni said he wanted us to be the 'perfect English family'; I was Daddy in a brown close-fitting suit from his menswear line, Bella was Mummy in a stiff on-the-knee dress and pearls, and Sophie was Baby in white chiffon.

Three minutes before we were due to go on Bella said, 'Jesus could this be any creepier?' I looked down at myself: every curve, every trace of feminity was obliterated. I couldn't do it. The playground taunts were going round in my head: *Her a model? She doesn't even look like a girl. She doesn't even look like a girl.*

'I'm not going on. I can't–I can't. It's horrible – ugly.' I was shaking and my voice was breaking up; another word and I'd lose it completely. Sophie's hands flew up to her face in horror; her eyes pleaded with me.

'Well, if you're sure, I'm game,' said Bella. 'I won't go on either.' She looked puzzled at the strength of my reaction, but quite pleased. I think she was looking forward to the row our rebellion would spark. Sophie was speechless.

'I'm sorry, Sophie – I can't do it. I just can't.' I started to unbutton my suit jacket. The Italian dresser – who only now began to understand what was afoot – reached out to stop me. When I shook her off, she turned and ran – to find Giovanni, I was sure. I was scared. I knew I was in big, big trouble. And I was getting Bella and Sophie in trouble too. Oh God, oh God.

And then a soft English voice said, 'You look wonderful you know.' It was Lucy Hayling – we'd never spoken but I knew her work and I'd envied her look: a classic blonde with elegant curves. No one would ever put her in a man's suit. She was wearing an exquisite silver dress. I remembered the running order of the show: she was due on just before us. She took my hand and looked into my eyes. 'Only the most beautiful women look good in men's clothes, and you do.' And she squeezed my hand.

'You really think so?' I whispered.

She nodded. 'You three – you'll bring the house down.'

'OK then,' I said, 'it's OK. I'm OK. Let's do it.' Sophie dropped her hands from her face and laughed – with nervous relief, I think. Bella said, 'Oh well, if we must. Let's get it over with.'

We took our positions at the entrance to the runway, Lucy immediately in front of us. I heard Giovanni shouting something in Italian, and then Lucy, her voice calm, amused: 'It's fine, Giovanni, fine. Everybody is happy.' Then the show director gave us our cue and we were on.

The audience loved us. Maybe our odd, mismatched appearance woke them up. I can still remember the noise that greeted our first few steps – a whoosh of surprise – a thousand people saying 'Ohh' – and then a ripple of laughter and finally huge waves of applause. Lucy was right: we made the show.

When Giovanni ran on to take his bow, he grabbed the three of us in a great hug – and then, somehow, propelled us to the end of the runway to share his moment. Lucy applauded with all the other models. I caught her eye, mouthed, 'Thank you.' She winked.

It was the last show in Milan Fashion Week.

'Hurry up!' snapped Bella at the dresser. The poor woman was having trouble working the zip on Bella's dress. Most of the backstage crew and models weren't in a hurry – at least not compared to the usual mad scramble. There were no other shows to go to, not today, not in Milan. But Bella clearly wanted out – out of the dress, out of Milan, out of fashion, I wasn't sure. After a week of shows she was in a dangerous mood.

Freed from the dress she cheered up. Suddenly she was in no hurry at all.

'Thank God. I thought my breasts had been taken hostage – so bloody uncomfortable,' and she raised her arms above her head and stretched. I looked away; she was completely naked. I shared a room with Sophie and had never yet seen her undressed; she was the type of girl who would change on the beach in an agony of embarrassment, wriggling under a towel. I wasn't as relaxed about nudity as Bella – I still didn't like getting stripped to a G-string in front of strangers – but it didn't kill me either; you get used to it. And that week in Milan, I discovered that the most beautiful girl in the world, in a G-string, is just a girl. Nobody really stood out.

Sophie was sitting at the make-up station, her back to the mirrors, waiting for Bella or me to make a move. She had taken all her make-up off and changed into her own clothes. I hadn't even noticed her doing it. She looked like a schoolgirl, out of uniform. Bella sat down next to Sophie. She peered into the mirror and said, 'Am I getting a spot on my chin? It's all the shitty make-up they make us wear.' She was still naked.

'Er, Bella, aren't you going to get dressed?' I said.

She looked up at me, mildly surprised.

'Oh yes, I forgot. I just get so sick of clothes, don't you?'

Bella was dressed by the time Giovanni put his arm round her and said, 'Ah, my English rose – my little English mama, so beautiful, beautiful . . .' He had somehow managed to get drunk within fifteen minutes of the show finishing, or maybe he had taken something, or maybe he had been drinking all day but pre-show nerves had kept him sober. I don't know. Bella looked like she was going to hit him. But then he said, 'You will come to my party tonight, yes? Very small, very intimate – just my closest friends. And bring your "husband"

and your "baby", yes?' Giovanni started to giggle. Bella smiled sweetly and said of course we were coming.

Giovanni's house was an hour's drive outside Milan. Bella's father gave us his car, and his driver, for the night. The inside of the Bentley was like a small luxurious room, a tiny gentleman's club filled with fine leather and wood. The three of us sat in our full-length silk dresses – on loan from the Giovanni's new collection, straight off the runway. The car moved so smoothly it hardly seemed to move at all.

There was a huge party in Milan that night, to mark the end of Fashion Week, but Bella said Giovanni's party was the place to be.

'He's a slug of a man, but he knows everybody. In the eighties he ran with a very fast crowd – you know, the survivors from the Andy Warhol factory, Studio 54 all that.' I had no idea what she was talking about. 'Daddy can't stand Giovanni, actually, and Mummy is even worse. She went quite loopy when she heard I had appeared in his show. I had her on speakerphone while I was getting dressed for tonight and, honestly, all the shouting was quite off-putting.' I wondered how she had persuaded her parents to let her go to Giovanni's tonight. 'Are we out of Milan yet?' asked Bella.

'Nearly,' said Sophie, 'another five minutes.'

Bella pressed the intercom button which connected the sound-proofed passenger area to the driver. 'Colin?'

'Yes, miss.'

'Change of plan. We're not going to Hetty's party after

all – it's bound to be deadly. Take us to . . .' And she gave him Giovanni's address.

'I don't know, miss, I think I should call your father first.'

'Don't be ridiculous, Colin. He doesn't like to be bothered with every little thing.' Colin protested but Bella wore him down. She promised we wouldn't stay any later than 2 a.m.

When the intercom was safely switched off, and the car was heading towards Giovanni's, I said, 'Bella . . .?'

She grinned. 'What they don't know can't hurt them. My parents think we're all going to my cousin Hetty's engagement party. She marrying some ghastly Italian – he's yonks older than her – at least thirty. I said I was dying to introduce you both to the happy couple.'

'But won't they find out?' said Sophie. 'I mean, when we don't turn up . . .'

'Well, yes – they probably will. But by the time they find out, it will be too late. Oh don't look so worried, you two – honestly! I just told a tiny fib so we could borrow the car. It's nothing. I mean, what harm can it do?'

We arrived at 10 p.m.

The driveway was lined on both sides with huge burning torches, planted into the ground; Sophie rolled a window down and leaned out; the cool night air rushed into the warm car.

'Oh, it's so pretty. Look – Jen, Bella, look how pretty it is!' I looked – just as the car turned a corner and the house came into view: it was so beautiful it didn't seem real. Pure white, with row upon row of shuttered windows, it might have been too stark in daylight but at night, its whiteness softened by the glow from the torches, the stone walls gave a curious illusion of softness; they could have been made from marshmallow.

Colin opened the car door for us and we got out, Bella leading the way. On the short walk to the house I was glad of the cold; I needed something to bring me to my senses. The car had lulled me into a dreamlike state that even Bella's brisk chatter had hardly disturbed. I could have curled up and slept on the smooth leather seats. It was nice, just the three of us, in our beautiful dresses and no one looking at us. But the moment we stepped out of the car my mood broke: we were three very dressed up models going to a designer's party.

An ordinary house party would have made me nervous enough, but Giovanni's 'very small' party was anything but ordinary. There must have been five hundred of his closest friends there, and the waiters were sprayed gold and dressed in loincloths and cherubs' wings.

For the first half hour I just stood in a corner with Sophie, holding on to my glass of champagne like it was a rope thrown to a drowning man. Or at least we would have stood in a corner if there had been any corners: the house must have had normal rooms once but Giovanni had scooped the insides out and then broken up the big empty spaces with walls that curved and rippled. There wasn't a straight line in the place. We leaned against a dip in a wall and watched Bella talking to a gorgeous boy who looked like he should be in an indie band.

'He is in a band,' whispered Sophie, though no one could have heard us above the din. 'Ricky Suzman – he's in Gentlemen Callers. I've got them on my iPhone. They're good, like the Arctic Monkeys, only better looking.' I'd never noticed Sophie liking music before; that she had a band I'd never heard of on her iPhone was an eye-opener. 'I didn't know Bella knew Ricky Suzman,' said Sophie. She sounded wistful.

'Maybe she'll bring him over,' I said.

Sophie was horrified. 'Oh no, I hope not, I'd die.'

I laughed and relaxed, a bit; if Mr Gentlemen Caller came over and spoke to us I was pretty sure I wouldn't die. Since starting modelling I'd been spoken to by several gorgeous guys – a few times I'd even managed to say something back. I thought of the *Clothes Crease* crowd, wondered if I'd see any of them again, wondered what Jack was doing . . .

'Oh no, you're right – she's bringing him over!' Sophie's panicked squeak dragged me back to the party.

'Jen, Sophie, this is Ricky – we were at school together.' We all said hello. I hoped Sophie would say something, she was the Gentlemen Callers' expert, after all, but she was staring at her feet. I glanced at her: her cheeks were as pink as her dress. There was nothing else for it.

'So, you're in a band . . . what's that like?'

Ricky Suzman looked at me like I was an idiot. I didn't blame him.

'Yeah, it's all right. It's been pretty mental lately, what with the tour 'n' all but like, you know . . .' His accent was totally weird – Cockney, I thought, mixed up with a bit of Mancunian or Scouse, it was hard to tell. And then it hit me: he was trying to sound working-class. Suddenly I wasn't so worried about making a prat of myself. Up close he wasn't so good-looking either, just really thin. People go on about models being anorexic but this boy was the thinnest person I had seen all week. Next to him Bella looked apple-cheeked and plump.

'Sophie is a big fan of your band, she says you're like the Arctic Monkeys only . . .' Sophie made an odd, choking noise, '. . . better.'

'Yeah?' He looked pleased.

'I've got your album,' said Sophie, quietly, shyly. 'It's really good.'

'Is it?' said Bella. 'The band are playing a set later – maybe I won't have to cover my ears after all. Ricky was rubbish at music at school; you should have heard him on the clarinet. I couldn't believe it when his band got signed. Oh good – canapés – I'm starving.' And with that she scooped three mini-pastries off a passing waiter's tray.

Sophie started going on about Ricky's album; she said several times it was 'brilliant' and 'really, really good'. I think she was trying to make up for Bella's rudeness but the more she went on the less interested Ricky looked. Finally he said he had to go and do a sound check with the band.

'C'mon, Bella,' and he draped an arm round her shoulders and led her off. Clearly he wasn't a bit put out by her low opinion of his musical ability. I wondered what it would be like to have so much charm you could say anything you liked and get away with it. Just before they disappeared into the crowd I saw him lean in close and whisper something in her ear; she threw her head back and laughed. I felt a bit bad for Sophie. Ricky Suzman had barely noticed her existence.

'We can't stand here all night, Sophie. Let's explore.'

I didn't know if the party was good or bad – I had nothing to compare it with – but it was fun just wandering through the crazy, curved rooms, looking at all the people. When I was a kid Aunt Pat took me and Bethany on a trip to a safari park; I pressed my face against the car window, scared at being so close to the lions, but excited too. That's how Giovanni's party was – there were a lot of big beasts.

We passed an old man in a dinner jacket and sunglasses, talking to a dark-haired model; the old man looked a lot like the actor Jack Nicholson – I'm pretty sure it *was* Jack Nicholson. There was a good-looking blonde couple who could have been Heath Ledger and Michelle Williams. I was almost a hundred per cent sure the guy was Heath Ledger but the girl might have been Kirsten Dunst.

All night I kept seeing famous people, but they were usually older, or fatter, or thinner, or plainer or prettier than I expected, so I was never quite sure. I remembered reading in *Heat* that Giovanni had dressed half of young Hollywood at last year's Oscars. Sophie didn't recognise anyone – in fact I got the distinct feeling that she hadn't even heard of a lot of the celebrities I thought I had spotted – so after a while I stopped asking her about them.

She was getting on my nerves, to be honest. She wasn't being difficult – the opposite in fact: she did everything I suggested. The problem was that she suggested nothing herself. If it had been up to Sophie, we would have stood like a couple of shop front dummies all night long. Which might have suited our host just fine.

Several times, people came up to us to get a closer look at our dresses; we got a lot of gushing compliments. The third time it happened I didn't bother to say, 'Grazie' – I realised that the praise was for Giovanni, not us. We weren't just wearing the dresses – we were *showing* them. By the time Giovanni himself came over, accompanied by a grey-haired woman dressed entirely in black, I knew what to expect. First he kissed us, then he told us we were beautiful, and then he said: 'Just turn round, girls, and let Helga see the back of the dresses.' We turned round and Helga gave a little gasp. She said something in German and then, in English: 'Genius, Giovanni, genius!'

When they were finished with us, Sophie – who had been on mineral water – accepted some pink champagne from a passing waiter. Our glasses full, we headed off to the marquee at the back of the house. We were just in time for the Gentlemen Callers.

Maybe Ricky couldn't play an instrument to save his life but it didn't matter: he was the lead singer. Up on the stage he looked beyond cool in his skinny black jeans and close-fitting suit jacket; he was wearing a tie I hadn't noticed earlier and carrying a briefcase. The rest of the band all looked like versions of Ricky.

The first song was called 'This Is What You Want, Come and Get It', or I think it was, because those were the only words I could make out. The music was hard and fast and quite good. The atmosphere should have been blinding but the crowd didn't really get going. For every five teen models or twenty-something actresses there was one bored middle-aged businessman or woman; the bored oldies acted like firebreaks, dampening down any excitement in the room. I tried to dance but it was hard, jumping up and down in high heels and a long dress. I looked around but I didn't see Bella. Maybe she couldn't be bothered watching her old school-friend perform. I wondered where she was. Sophie didn't take her eyes off Ricky.

At the end of their set – the band only played for half an hour – Ricky snarled into the microphone: 'This is what you want – come and get it.' Then he opened the briefcase and tipped the contents into the crowd. Sheets of paper fluttered down; I pulled one out of Sophie's hair; it was a hundred dollar bank-note – printed with Ricky's face.

116

'Why?' said Sophie, mystified.

I stared at the fake money in my hand. 'I think it's some sort of statement,' I replied, 'you know – we're all shallow money-grabbing bastards and the band are above all that. Or something.'

'Oh. How rude.'

I laughed. Sometimes Sophie was so sweet, so innocent, she made me feel older, experienced. It was a nice change from feeling like a stupid kid out of my depth. I put my arm round her.

'Come on, Soph – let's go for a swim.'

We had passed the pool on our way to the marquee; I'd almost stopped then, it had looked so inviting, the steam from the heated water rising into the cold night air. There were changing rooms at the side of the pool, and attendants handing out complimentary swimwear and towels.

'I don't think I want to go for a swim,' said Sophie. 'It's late. You don't go swimming at night.'

'They are,' I said, nodding towards the people in the pool. (They weren't actually swimming – they were standing, and drinking champagne, but they were in the water.) Sophie just shook her head and I knew she wouldn't be persuaded.

'Well I'm going in,' I said, though by now I didn't really want to, not on my own.

I collected a black bikini from the attendant and got changed, feeling nervous. As soon as I was in the water I relaxed; it was as hot as a bath. I lay on my back and looked up at the stars. A light, female voice floated across the water: 'So I told the director, don't even think I'm signing up for this dumb-ass film unless I get to work with Leo DiCaprio . . .' I couldn't believe that this was my life.

After about fifteen minutes of floating and dreaming I started to feel bad about leaving Sophie on her own with no one to talk to. I glanced over at her; she was sitting on a poolside lounger and she wasn't alone. A dark-haired man was sitting next to her, very close. He was talking to her and she was smiling. I stood up; suddenly I was wide awake: it must be nearly 2 a.m., I thought, Colin would be looking for us.

I waded over to the side of the pool and hauled myself out. A bored-looking attendant handed me a towel. Sophie didn't even look over. I called out that I was going to get changed and we needed to go. The man turned round: he gave a look that made me shiver – I felt assessed, taken in, in an instant. I had been judged on my looks all week but this was different, it was personal. I walked to the changing room knowing that I wasn't his type. Sophie was his type. She was sixteen and looked younger; he was at least thirty-five. What on earth were they talking about? I couldn't imagine.

I stepped into my dress, hardly taking time to dry myself. We had ten minutes to find Bella and make it to the car. When I came out, Sophie was standing up and obviously ready to go. To my relief, it looked like she was binning the old guy. I hung back – I didn't want to have to meet him, speak to him. He handed her something; she took it, giggled, put it in her clutch bag. Then he kissed her on the mouth and went back into the house. I rushed over.

'He kissed you! What did he give you?'

'His number.' She held her head up and looked me in the eye. I was shocked.

'Sophie, he's geriatric You're not actually going to see him again?'

'Why not? And he's not that old, he's – mature. I'm tired of boys. Guido says men under thirty don't know how to treat a woman – they don't appreciate their intelligence. He says the way I speak Italian is charming.' I was going to argue but then I thought, what's the point? We were leaving tomorrow – she would never see him again anyway. So I said we didn't have time to stand around talking, which was true. We had to find Bella.

Twenty minutes later, after a frantic and fruitless search, we ran into Colin on the steps of the house.

'Where is she?' He looked tired and his voice was tight with anger. I was still glad to see him. He was an adult, he worked for Bella's father – let him find her. He did – in Giovanni's garage.

She was peering into the engine of a silver sports car; there must have been at least ten other cars in the garage – it was like a showroom. A few guests from the party – all men – were milling about, watched closely by attendants in silver overalls. Obviously Giovanni's cars were one of the party's attractions. Colin marched over to Bella. Sophie and I followed at a safe distance.

'One of these days, Bella, you are going to cost me my job.' I noticed that Colin had dropped the 'miss'. 'Your father's been on the phone. He's not happy. Neither am I.'

Bella stood up straight and closed the bonnet of the car.

'I'm sorry, Colin. I'll speak to him – you shouldn't get the blame. I'll make sure you don't.' Colin didn't say anything but the expression on his face softened. 'What do you think?' said Bella, nodding towards the silver car.

'Your father has the 1962 model, miss. I believe it's generally thought superior.'

Bella yawned.

'Oh Daddy has the best of everything. Don't be cross, Colin, I know it's time to go. I've seen what I came for.' She strolled over and linked arms with me and Sophie. 'Daddy says the only good thing about Giovanni is his vintage car collection; I've been dying to see it. When he offered us an invite to his stupid party I couldn't say no, could I? Was it boring? Did you meet any cute guys?' Sophie blushed. She gave me a look: *please, don't.*

'No, no cute guys,' I said. 'Nobody at all.'

14

'You didn't put the bins out, did you? I told you, last night, I said, "Make sure you put the bins out, it's collection in the morning," and you didn't bloody bother. And now it'll be two weeks – two weeks – before the binmen will be round again. We'll get rats – *rats!*' Mum was shaking with rage; it had been a while since she'd been like this. I didn't think it would be a good idea to point out that I was on the phone.

'Sorry, Mum – I forgot.' Keep it simple. No point mentioning that I'd been travelling all day yesterday and had got home knackered.

'Oh you forgot, did you? Head too full of modelling, I suppose, and Milan and all those poncy designers telling you how bloody beautiful you are. Well you don't look like much from where I'm standing, let me tell you. Pat's right – her Bethany is the only one with looks in this family.' And she stormed out of my bedroom, slamming the door behind her.

I picked up my phone: 'Corinne? Hi, yeah, sorry about that, Mum needed a word. Yes – you're right, it is time I moved to London. And I'd love to share a flat with Sophie and Bella.'

My homecoming had not been a great success. Let's just say Mum didn't put out any flags. I did have an unexpected visitor though, on the day I got back: my cousin Bethany came round to ask me about Milan. I showed her some pictures I'd taken with my phone – a couple of touristy shots of the Duomo but mostly just Sophie and Bella backstage at the shows – and she said how exciting it all looked, and how great it must be to get away.

'Sophie is really pretty, isn't she?' said Bethany, tracing her finger across the tiny screen. I was sure she was thinking, not like you – I can see why Sophie is a model, but you? How did that ever happen? But if Bethany was thinking anything like that she hid it really well.

'I'm sorry about Mum, you know, the way she's been behaving.' For a minute I thought she meant *my* mum, but then I realised, of course – Aunt Pat. I still didn't know what she was going on about. Come to think of it, I hadn't set eyes on Aunt Pat for months. 'I mean, it's so stupid of her to avoid you, but she's just a bit – embarrassed. I don't think she means any harm.'

'Embarrassed? About what?'

'You making it as a model of course. After going on for years about how I would end up a cover girl, she doesn't know what to say to you.' Bethany rolled her eyes as if to say, mums eh? What can you do with them? 'I tried to tell her that I didn't have the looks for modelling, but she just wouldn't let it go.' Bethany looked up at me with her lovely blue eyes; she was right – she was pretty in a real-life, girl-next-door way; but I knew the industry well enough now to know that this wasn't enough. She didn't look like a model. I said I was sorry.

'Don't be – I'm not. I must be the only girl in my class at school who doesn't want to be famous. I want to be a vet. I just have to work out a way of persuading Mum that being good at science and maths isn't a tragedy.'

'Do you think we could swap mums?' I said. 'Only mine thinks modelling is rubbish and that I look like shit.' I meant it as a joke but the way it came out, it wasn't funny. I flipped my phone open for no reason, and then shut it again.

'Our mums are nutters,' said Bethany. I burst out laughing. 'You are a brilliant model, I'm going to be a vet, and that's that. They're just going to have to get used to it.'

As soon as Bethany had gone I phoned Stevie.

Somehow, because my cousin had been nice to me, it was easier to make the call. I didn't feel quite so alone. The feeling that everybody in my home town hated me had lifted, just enough for me to take a risk. If he rang off without speaking, if he told me he hated me, I would be able to bear it. I didn't think any of this at the time, I just picked up the phone and made the call. He answered immediately.

'Hi. It's me.' I didn't give him time to say anything. If he said the wrong thing, if he was off with me, we might have another row; I had to get my apology out – fast. 'I've been an idiot, Stevie. The things I said at the bus stop, I didn't mean them – I'm sorry, I'm really, really sorry.' There was silence. My stomach dropped. I thought: oh God, he's not going to forgive me – I'm going to leave town and move to London and I'm never going to see him again. And then:

'Of course I forgive you, you freak. You left school – big deal. I would too if I had half a chance. Come round right now. And you better have got me a present from duty free.'

'God, you took your time. Is that Hugo Boss?' I nodded. Stevie grabbed the bottle of men's cologne out of my hand and said, 'Wait here. *He's* back and it's all kicking off with Mum. I'll just put this under my bed and then we can clear off.' And he shut the door in my face. I wondered, for one horrible moment, if Stevie was playing a sick joke on me. Maybe he hadn't forgiven me – maybe he just wanted to make me suffer. But no, it was all right, a few seconds later he was back, wearing his favourite black jacket and a beanie hat I didn't recognise.

'Fancy seeing a film?' he said, as he shut the door behind him.

'Yeah,' I said, 'course I do.' It was like I had never been away, like nothing had happened.

The bus stop was deserted: it was cold and windy; cars crawled past. I thought suddenly of the last time we were together at a bus stop; the thought made me nervous. On the bus we went up to our usual spot – upstairs, right at the front.

'So did you go all the way into town to get me the Hugo Boss from Boots?' I was startled at how pissed off he sounded. I took a deep breath and owned up.

'Yeah, yeah I did. I was late for my flight and I didn't have time to shop at the airport. Sorry, I should have said . . .' He nodded but didn't speak and then he was laughing – laughing so hard I had to sit there like a muppet waiting for him to catch his breath before he could speak. Eventually, he wiped his eyes and grinned.

'I knew as soon as I said I was expecting a present that you would go charging into town and panic buy me a monster bottle of Hugo Boss. Priceless!'

I threw every swear word I could think of at him, but I wasn't really angry. I was so relieved I could have cried. If he was taking the piss out of me then that had to mean things were really OK between us, didn't it?

We went to the multiplex cinema in the mall. It was always a pretty safe bet – a good place to kill some time, when things at home were getting rough. We liked sitting in the dark, and the salted popcorn. The multiplex had six screens. Screen six was so small I swear Stevie's dad had brought home bigger TVs. But screen six was ours. It showed films so bad they should have gone straight to video and films so odd they were almost arty; once or twice we even saw something with subtitles. ('As if anyone in this town can even *read*,' said Stevie.) No one ever bothered us in screen six; just occasionally we would bump into someone's parents. Stevie spotted his great-gran once, watching a Judi Dench period drama and wearing a jaunty purple hat. She bought us ice creams afterwards and said we made a lovely couple. But today it was empty.

We watched two films, back to back: a romcom set in Paris – American geek falls in love with wacky French girl – and a comedy about a retirement home in Brighton. The retirement home film was slightly better even though all the main characters died at the end; everybody who was still alive had a party on the beach where they got drunk and smoked a lot of marijuana, for medical reasons.

'That was such a good way to spend four hours,' said Stevie, as we emerged, blinking, into the foyer. 'I'm so glad we didn't waste the afternoon writing a novel or working for world peace.'

'I missed you,' I said. Stevie went a bit pink and told me, 'Don't be soft.' But what I really meant was, 'I should have missed you.' Because I hadn't thought of him, not much, anyway, in Milan. The moment I was back home, Stevie – and the row we'd had – was a really big deal. But there was so much else to think about when I was working, maybe I'd blocked him out.

Standing in the foyer, watching him pick flecks of popcorn off his jacket, I couldn't believe that I hadn't wanted him with me in Milan. There was no one like him – no one as clever or funny. Sophie and Bella . . . they seemed far away from me now. I hadn't even mentioned their names to Stevie; it was like I'd been cheating on him.

Then he said, 'Why did you fork out for the tickets and the popcorn and the drinks? We always go halves.'

I thought: isn't it obvious? 'I'm earning now, that's all.'

'Right – yeah, I suppose so. So, are you making a lot

then?' I glanced around the Odeon foyer. Why did we have to have this conversation here? I'd never noticed how brash, how ugly it was. The electric blue carpet had built-in strips of flashing lights.

'Yeah, quite a bit – I think so.' I chose my words carefully. 'But most of it goes into a trust fund until I'm eighteen. Until then I just get an allowance – you know, like pocket money.' I hoped he wouldn't asked me how much 'pocket money' I got, because it was a lot. He didn't. We were squeezed against a wall in the foyer; crowds of people were pouring in for the early evening showings. Stevie was right under a huge Vin Diesel poster. Under normal circumstances he would have found Vin looming over him funny. At last, he started to move towards the door.

'Well, at least you didn't empty your piggy bank to buy me the Hugo Boss. Next time you can buy me a suit, not a poxy bottle of perfume.' I think he was trying to be funny but I didn't laugh. We were out on the street. We walked for a couple of minutes. I wasn't sure where we were going. 'I don't mind you being minted,' said Stevie. I wished he would stop going on about money. 'I think it's great – really I do. You deserve it. It's just . . . odd, that's all. It'll take a bit of getting used to.'

From then on we were a little bit careful with each other. Neither of us risked any cutting jokes; we were – polite. Despite all the politeness the money thing came up again, in McDonald's.

'Are you sure you want to eat here?'

'Of course I am,' I said, irritated and not able to hide it. 'Just because I've got some money in my pocket it doesn't make me the Queen. I'm not a millionaire you know.'

'No . . . I meant – do you fancy a kebab instead? You said you were getting fed up with fish burgers, remember?'

'Oh.' I tried to smile. 'No, thanks, I'm really in the mood for a burger. Can't beat it. And anyway – you're paying.' I don't know what I was thinking. That last bit, it just jumped out of my mouth before I had time to engage my brain.

Stevie stared. 'Actually, things are a bit tight at home. Can we just pay for our own as usual?'

On the bus going home we were both pretty quiet. I didn't want to say anything in case I stuck my foot in it again. I wasn't sure what was going on in Stevie's head. As the bus got closer to my stop, I started to panic about telling him I was moving to London. It wouldn't have been easy, even earlier in the day when were getting on so well, but now, after a couple of crappy hours, I didn't know how to get the words out. I was afraid he wouldn't care. But if I went without telling him, that would be worse than anything.

'Stevie – I spoke to Corinne this morning and we agreed it is time for me—'

'It's you, isn't it?' I looked up. Two girls, about twelve or thirteen, were staring at me. 'You're that model, from our school.' I admitted that yes, it was me. Stevie was looking out of the window. The girls didn't seem to have anything else to say, but they didn't go back to their seats either. They just stood there, gawping.

Eventually the slightly taller one said, 'I really like your hair. Has it always been that short?' I said no, no it hadn't; I used to wear it quite long.

'Really?' said her friend. 'Was it as long as mine?' Her hair reached the top of her low-slung jeans. I said no, mine wasn't quite as long as that.

Stevie twisted round in his seat.

'Would you two like her autograph?'

The girls beamed. 'Yeah – that'd be great.'

He pulled a notebook out of his man-bag; he carried the notebook everywhere with him. Whenever he was bored he would make sketches, quite often of the person who was boring him. He tore out two pages and handed them to me.

'Here – you can write on the back.' He gave me a pen. On one of the pages he'd drawn a caricature of the headmaster; it reduced his beady little eyes to pin-pricks; on the other was a simple sketch of his little brother, sitting on the floor, his head bent over a raggedy-looking bear. Stevie was very private about his drawings; he didn't even show them to me very often. I was speechless.

'Haven't you got any plain paper?' said the taller girl.

'No I haven't,' said Stevie. 'You can take it or leave it.' I scribbled my name on the back of Stevie's drawing, just to get it over with.

The girls went back to their seats. The bus turned into the road at the end of my street. I had two minutes to tell him I was moving to London. I bottled it.

'I'll see you, Stevie.' Then I rang the bell and got off the bus.

I was walking quickly, almost running, when I felt someone grab my arm. I turned round: Stevie.

'What are you doing? Why did you get off the bus?'

He shrugged. 'I'll walk home. I could do with the exercise.'

'Stevie – I should have told you this earlier. I'm moving to London.'

'I know,' he said. 'I mean, I didn't know for sure, but I thought you would. Why wouldn't you? It makes sense. Your work is in London. There's nothing for you here.'

'You're here.'

He smiled, but it was the sort of smile that doesn't reach the eyes. 'I know, but I'm not going anywhere. We can visit. It'll be all right, it will.'

I was so rattled, I didn't even feel relief. I said, without much enthusiasm, 'I'm not going till Saturday, that means we've still got tomorrow to hang out. Shall I come round to yours – do a DVD box set?'

He shook his head. 'I'm sorry, I can't, not tomorrow. I've got plans.'

'Yeah, right,' I said. 'Of course you do.'

'What do you mean by that?' he snapped. For the second time today I was taken aback at how angry he sounded; only this time, I was sure the anger was real. Well, I was pretty pissed off too.

'What I mean is that you've been blowing hot and cold

with me all bloody day. One minute you couldn't be nicer and the next you're giving me a really hard time. Don't just pretend that everything is all right if you're still in a strop with me, OK? At least be honest.' He tried to say something, but I wouldn't let him. 'It's not my fault that those girls wanted my autograph. *And I don't have to apologise for being successful!*' I gave him a shove. I just wanted him out of my face but I was so worked up I pushed him harder than I meant to. He stumbled backwards and fell – right on his arse. 'Stevie! I'm sorry . . .' I reached out my hand to help him up but he slapped it away.

'Shut up! Just shut up, can't you?' He got to his feet and brushed the back of his jeans with his hand. 'God you are so full of yourself!' I was breathing so fast, I couldn't speak.

Two men walked past, clutching cans of lager. 'Lovers' tiff, eh?' said one, and the other laughed and said, 'Why don't you try someone your own size, love? A real man.'

Stevie stared at the men, his fists clenched, until they were out of sight. Then he said, 'You have the nerve to talk about "honesty". You don't tell me anything about your life any more. I don't have a clue what you did in Milan. We've been together all day and you've hardly mentioned it. What's the matter? Don't you think I can take it? "Poor Stevie can't bear to hear about my great new life!" Is that it? Is that what you think?'

'I don't know what to think,' I screamed back. 'I don't know what to say! Leave me alone!' I was close to tears. Maybe Stevie saw it in my face, because his expression

131

changed, softened just a fraction, and he stepped towards me.

'Jen . . .'

I stepped back.

'Don't, Stevie – just don't. I don't want to fight with you. I don't want to make up. I just want to go home.' And I turned and fled.

I spent my last night at home in my bedroom, avoiding Mum, listening to music and packing everything I owned into the Prada luggage I'd picked up in a discount store in Milan.

Mum knew I was leaving for good on Saturday ('Look after yourself,' was all she said) but I forgot to tell her I'd booked a cab for 9 a.m. I was trying so hard not to think about Stevie, I couldn't think straight about anything else. So when the cab arrived, Mum was at the corner shop, buying milk. She was always running out of milk. I left a note on the kitchen table: 'Gone to London. I'll phone when I get there. Jen. x'

The cab passed her. She was hurrying back from the shop, holding the milk and a large bag of croissants close to her chest. Even as a kid, I'd liked croissants better than cake. I think she must have bought them for me. I thought of asking the driver to pull over but then the traffic lights changed to green and suddenly it was too late, she was gone. And I was crying and I didn't know who I was crying for.

15

'Which one of you bitches has taken my Factor 40?'

Natalie was in a filthy mood. She had been in a filthy mood since the day she moved into the flat, almost two months ago, and discovered that a flat share involved a lot of *sharing*. Natalie didn't like to 'share'; she thought it was a poncy word for stealing other people's stuff. On this occasion she was shaking with rage and, as usual at times of emotional stress, naked. To be fair, she was actually wearing knickers and a hand towel; unfortunately the towel was wrapped around her hair. I sank deeper into the sofa and wondered why she couldn't be angry and wear clothes at the same time. Even Sophie didn't bother averting her eyes any more. She was gazing up at Natalie, perfectly unembarrassed. Bella was flicking through a motoring magazine.

'I've got a job tomorrow and I've been told not to turn up with a tan. It's thirty degrees outside! So where is my bloody Factor 40? None of you bitches are going anywhere until I've got my Factor 40!'

'Mmm, Natalie – where did you last see your sunblock?' asked Sophie.

'In the bedroom.' The effort of thinking crawled across Natalie's face. 'Yeah, it was definitely somewhere in the bedroom.'

'Maybe it's still there,' suggested Sophie. 'Would you like some help looking for it?'

Natalie considered. 'Yeah, all right. Thanks, Soph.'

Sophie got up, gave Natalie a consoling pat on the arm, and they headed off to the bedroom Natalie shared with Freda, a German girl I had never actually spoken to because she spent so much time chatting on MySpace.

'You know, if we could extract Sophie's calming influence and inject it into Natalie every day, she might actually be sane,' I said.

'Oh she's not that bad,' said Bella, taking a bite out of a green apple.

'She is that bad – you're not here all the time, you don't know how bad it gets.' Bella spent a lot of weekends at her parents' place in the country. She also had a suite at her father's London hotel, which she used whenever she fancied.

'You know you can stay at the hotel any time you like if you need a break from the madness. Daddy won't mind.' No, I thought, but I'd mind. I'd been living in London for four months and I liked paying my own way. My old schoolgirl life of Saturday jobs and pocket money and 'as long as you're under my roof you'll abide by my rules' seemed a million miles away. I was independent now. I was nearly seventeen. I didn't need any favours from anybody's dad.

Bella had refused to let her dad buy her a flat but he was always doing things for her. When she mentioned the fridge had broken down, he sent round a new one on the same day, along with a hamper from Harrods' food hall, and a chef, who cooked us dinner. ('Poor Daddy,' said Bella, breaking a lobster's claw in two, 'he can't bear the idea of me roughing it.')

And he didn't just buy her stuff; he spent time with her. About once a month he took her with him on a business trip – usually to Tokyo or New York. At weekends they worked together, restoring a vintage car he had had shipped over from Belgium. I said once that she must be really looking forward to turning seventeen and being able to drive. 'Oh I drive all the time when I'm at home,' she said. 'It's perfectly legal as long as I stick to the estate and avoid the public highways. Daddy taught me, when I was twelve.'

Living with Bella, and seeing how big a part her dad played in her life, made me wonder what – or who – I'd been missing. I had never known my dad, and never wanted to either. But if fathers thought their daughters were so wonderful, why had I been so easy to leave?

Suddenly there was a yelp of joy: 'My Factor 40! You found it!'

'This really is a very good apple,' said Bella, taking another bite and munching. 'Daddy's right – Mummy is a wonderful gardener. He keeps offering to set her up in an organic fruit business but she doesn't seem keen for some reason. Here . . .' she picked up a brown paper bag from the floor and pulled out another apple, 'try one.'

It was the hottest summer I could remember. Or maybe summers were always hotter in London, I didn't know, it was my first. I was busy with work – editorial shoots for magazines, and more and more advertising campaigns – and for the first time in my life I also had a busy social life. I had a life.

It was a summer of terrace parties and barbeques and standing around in fashion students' scruffy kitchens with plastic glasses of lukewarm wine. I met hundreds of people and they were all in the fashion business, or wanted to be.

I was starting to become well known. *Clothes Crease in Hot Cars* came out in May and the cover image – me feeding Francine cherry pie – created a lot of buzz. People I met for the first time already knew who I was. On shoots I was 'fantastic' and 'amazing' before the first photograph had been taken. Everybody loved my work. I got used to being told I was 'the new Agyness Deyn' even though I looked nothing like her.

I didn't admit it to anybody – I hardly admitted it to myself – but I liked being *asked* to parties more than I liked partying. On a shoot everybody had a job to do and I knew how to do mine. But hanging out with a crowd of people after the shoot, everything was a lot more complicated. I didn't know the rules and there was no expert I could go to who could teach me how to behave. The agency had sorted out my hair and my walk (not to mention my nails, eyebrows and bikini line) but when it came to after-hours activities I was on my own. Except for Sophie.

Sophie didn't get as many bookings as I did, so she was usually free when I needed her company. I'd text her the address where I was going to be, with a crowd of people after work, and she'd turn up.

No doorman or bar staff ever asked to see my ID; the crowd I was with were usually all over eighteen and, besides, being so tall made me look older. Sophie looked about fourteen so she was turned away from a lot of clubs. If I was already inside she would text me, ID and I'd make my excuses and leave. She was always very apologetic, but I didn't mind, usually. Sophie's baby face got me out of a lot of dull clubs.

We would go back to the flat and watch DVDs or go out for pizza. Once we went to a really corny American-style diner and had milkshakes and burgers and pretended to be teenagers in the 1950s. Bella joined us, and, getting into the spirit of things, kept shouting, 'Great balls of fires!' I don't know what that had to do with the fifties but it made us laugh.

In a crowd of strangers Sophie smiled a lot and laughed when anybody made a joke but she didn't say much. Looking back, I don't think any of my brand-new friends minded, or even noticed, but somehow in my head it was a problem. It was like I had to cover for her – make conversation for two.

I'd hear myself going on and on about some incident at the shoot, which wasn't even that funny, and then I'd start to worry that I was being overbearing, and I'd clam up. After five or ten minutes of sitting quietly I'd worry that everyone would think I was in a strop, so then I'd burst into life again. Having a good time could be pretty tiring.

I didn't drink much (the memory of waking up on Zac's bathroom floor was still too vivid) and Sophie hardly drank at all. It didn't matter how lairy a party got, or how many people were off their heads, we were OK. The truth is, little Sophie made me feel safe. I'm not sure exactly what it was I needed protecting from – maybe just the newness of living and working in London, the strangeness. I needed time to catch up with my life.

That summer I went out a lot and nothing bad happened. (Was it really only last year? I can hardly believe it.) People think the fashion scene is full of drugs and sleaze but I didn't see anything that freaked me out. The one time we got out of our depth it wasn't anything to do with the fashion business. It was all the fault of rock 'n' roll.

The Waiting had just reached number one in the US album charts. The band had been around for years, but for some reason they were only just becoming big. I had a small part in the video for the band's latest single. The video shoot took two days and was a lot of fun. I got to lie in a coffin, acting dead; I thought of *CSI* and tried to make it realistic. At the end of the video I came back to life and chased the lead singer through a graveyard. We had to do about thirty takes because he couldn't stop laughing. It was classic Buffy meets cheesy 1980s video.

The band were almost comically polite; their accents reminded me of Francine Hope. All the Americans on the set called me 'Miss Jones'. It was a laugh.

When the lead singer asked me to go to a party to celebrate the album's success, I thought, why not?

I called Sophie, as usual, and we arrived at the Camden address together. Straightaway it didn't feel right. I expected the house to be spectacular and it was – spectacularly shabby. Outside the paint was peeling from the walls and inside there was a really odd smell of something unwashed and old. It didn't matter which room we stood in we couldn't get away from it. Apart from the other models from the video, everybody there was much older than us; nobody was dancing. A lot of people were sitting around looking completely out of it. There was no sign of the band.

I said we didn't have to stay long and Sophie said it was fine, really.

A strikingly pale model waved at me from the other side of the room. She was slumped in a massive, battered-looking armchair. I waved back, just to be polite. I had never even spoken to her at the video shoot; she had spent the whole two days draped around the drummer, being his vampire girlfriend. To my surprise, she hauled herself out of the chair and came over. The idea of having to talk to her was alarming.

'Hey – would you like some?' She offered us a swig from her bottle of Jack Daniels. Her face was pale and clammy and she looked like she had had enough.

'No thanks,' I said.

'Very sensible. I bet you're working tomorrow, aren't you?' She didn't give me time to reply. 'Yeah, I bet you are. You are so hot right now. Sexy girls – girls with tits – we can't get a break. What do you think of my breasts?' She was wearing a dress so low-cut it looked like a nipple might escape at any moment.

'Great,' I said, 'they're very nice.'

'Four grand they cost me. That's two grand per tit. I'm still paying for them. How much work do you think they've got me? Go on – guess.'

'Er, I don't know – a lot?'

'Nada – nothing. Fashion sucks, it's such bullshit. There's no market for real women.'

She lifted the bottle and nearly drained it. I wanted to be somewhere else so badly, it was like a physical ache. But somehow I couldn't move. I had no idea how to get away from someone at a party without causing offence.

'You're pretty.' The model reached out and stroked Sophie's hair. Sophie flinched. 'So pretty . . .' she said again, and took another swig of whisky. 'Want some?' When we refused she up-ended the bottle into my glass; most of the whisky ran over my hand. I stepped back, shocked. She dropped the empty bottle on the floor.

'The guys in the band are so cool, don't you think? They're

so real. They're real men. And that's what I need. I don't have any time any more for loser fashion creeps. I just don't have any time to waste. I'm going to get a real man,' and she turned and walked, in a surprisingly straight line, back to the armchair. She sat down, carefully, and closed her eyes.

'Oh my God – what is she like?' I said.

'I think,' said Sophie, as though there was any doubt about it, 'she's had a bit too much to drink.'

It looked like the band had decided to skip their own party. Maybe that's why it was so scuzzy and lame. The party had a big hole in the centre. There were a lot of hangers-on with nothing to hang on to.

When the director of the video came over I was relieved. He had been nice to work with – calm, professional. He said I had been great to work with ('you British chicks are so cool'). Then he asked if we would like to join him upstairs for a 'private party'. I wasn't sure exactly what he meant but I knew enough to say 'no'. He didn't seem particularly bothered. I saw him glance round the room; there were two other models standing in a corner; they looked a little bit older than us. 'Whatever. Your loss,' he said, and headed off in their direction.

'Jen, if it isn't too early for you, do you think we could . . .'

'Get the hell out of here?'

'Go home, yes.'

'Yeah – good idea. Just let's find a bathroom so I can wash this booze off my hands.'

The bathroom door wasn't locked. We walked straight in – and saw the lead singer of The Waiting pushing a needle into the drummer's arm. They were crouched over the toilet. I said, 'Sorry,' and we walked out and kept walking until we were in the street.

Sophie flagged down the first black cab that came along. I was glad, I didn't want to face the night bus. I didn't want to be around people.

If you've had a top night, travelling home through late night London is a kind of a rush. I used to love the sense that the night wasn't over until my head hit the pillow; anything could happen. But when you've had a rubbish night and you just want to be home, the journey is like a maths test on a Monday morning. It can't be over soon enough.

After the Camden party I didn't even want to be in the cab. I wished we had a Tardis that could land us in the flat in seconds. But if we'd had a Tardis I would set the coordinates so that we went back in time a few hours and never went to the stupid party in the first place.

'It's OK, Jen,' said Sophie, 'it's not your fault. Those people were just . . .'

'. . . a bunch of sleazy druggies?'

Sophie smiled. 'Yes, I suppose they were. They were so much older than us – maybe it's just, you know, a generation thing.'

I thought of the old guy, Guido, at the Giovanni's party in Rome. The generation gap didn't seem to bother her then. Then I felt bad about even thinking that when Sophie was being so nice. She was always nicer to me than I deserved. I didn't deserve her.

I put my head on Sophie's shoulder. When I sat up again we were driving through Islington. It was quiet; there were no drunks on the streets, the streets were almost empty. I wanted to say, 'Are we nearly there yet?' but I stopped myself because only kids say that.

It was so nice to be home. The relief made me feel almost elated. The flat *was* home – despite all the rows and the endless succession of deranged flatmates. Sophie made some toast and we ate it on the sofa. I found Natalie's Factor 40 behind a cushion. 'Oh crap,' I said, 'she's gone out without it.' Sophie giggled. The toast was warm and buttery; it was the best toast I had ever tasted.

We heard a key turn in front door: Bella – just back from Tokyo.

'Great,' she said, 'toast. Budge up,' and she squeezed in between us and took a slice from my plate. 'So what have you two been up to? How was the rock stars' party? Have I just missed the party of the century? Why are you laughing? What? What's funny?'

16

As summer faded into autumn, I saw less of Sophie and Bella. We still shared the flat but our schedules were so different we weren't often able to get together. To Corinne's increasing exasperation Bella spent more and more time at her parents' place in the country. Now that she was seventeen, and able to drive on 'public highways', she took off whenever she felt like it, driving the three hundred miles from Hoxton to Cornwall as though she was just nipping to the corner shop. Clients had to practically beg her to work for them. Once, in the middle of a shoot for a designer's accessories line, she went to the loo and didn't come back. ('I don't know why everyone is so cross about it,' she told me later. 'I rolled about naked on that set for two hours, the photographer got hundreds of pictures. I didn't mind the nudity but I had to cover my bits the whole time with a bloody handbag!')

I was working so hard I didn't have the time to hang out in clubs or go to many parties. Instead of one job a day there would be three or four – and the days were getting longer: 5 a.m. starts and 3 a.m. finishes became normal. In November

I went three weeks without setting eyes on Sophie. When we finally bumped into each other – at 4 a.m. in the bathroom – I asked her where she had been. I assumed she had been working overseas. 'I haven't been anywhere,' she said. 'I haven't worked for two weeks. I've been here the whole time. You're the one who has been away.' From anyone else this would have sounded resentful, jealous, but there was no edge in Sophie's voice. All she was doing was pointing out a simple fact: I was working a lot more than she was.

Models between jobs can be a pain in the bum. Several of the girls who stayed at the flat had a lot of free time; they tended to spend it watching TV, bitching on the phone to their other out-of-work model friends, and getting off with boys. The delightful Katya from the Ukraine had a talent for doing all three at the same time – usually on the living-room sofa. ('The multi-tasker', Bella called her.)

Sophie was different. She was always usefully occupied. A cleaner employed by the agency came to the flat for two hours once a week but there was never anything for her to do; Sophie kept the place shining. 'Most model flats I work in are pigsties – no offence, dear,' said Mary, the cleaner, 'but that girl cleans like a professional. I said to her, "You ever get fed up with modelling, come and talk to me. We could set up in business together." '

I was surprised when Sophie took up running – anyone less sporty-looking it was hard to imagine – but she turned out to be a natural. The first time I saw her run, I almost didn't recognise her. I was stuck in traffic, on the way to the airport. She sprinted past my cab with a long, elegant stride that seemed to belong to someone else. On the runway she was always a little awkward.

When she wasn't cleaning or running she was studying. She did a lot of online courses. The only one I really took any notice of was German language for business travellers. She supplemented the lessons with DVDs of German films. I walked in on her watching *Das Boot* with her eyes closed ('so I don't read the English subtitles').

I was impressed at how busy Sophie kept herself. I thought it meant that she was coping well with the temporary downturn in her career.

I did wonder, though, why she didn't visit her family in Suffolk more often. After all, when work picked up again it would be hard for her to get away. 'Mum says I have to be available at short notice – show the agency I'm committed to my career. As long as Focus wants to keep me in London, then I should stay in London. She says I haven't lost my looks yet, so I just need to work on my attitude.' I thought Sophie's mum sounded like a right cow.

At least my mum didn't bend my ear with unwanted career advice. I would text her occasionally just to let her know where I was in case she needed to contact me. My texts weren't exactly chatty, I admit ('In Paris 4 job. Back Tuesday. x' was fairly typical) but her replies were hardly gushing either ('OK. Mum x').

Me moving out had not changed our relationship for the worse. True, those moments of mother-daughter bonding

146

didn't happen any more. (There *were* some, believe it or not: we used to watch made-for-TV movies. We both liked the ones where women were duped into marrying murderers.) But on the other hand she wasn't shouting at me through my bedroom door. Which was an improvement. So on balance, we were as close as we'd ever been.

I was surprised when Mum phoned – actually phoned, instead of emailing or texting – to ask me if I was coming home for my seventeenth birthday in December.

'Why?' I said. 'Is Aunt Pat baking a cake?'

'Pat's not in a cake-baking mood. Bethany's refusing to go to any more acting or modelling auditions. Says she wants to go to university and study to be a vet. Pat's gutted. Says she never thought a daughter of hers would make a living sticking her hand up cows' bottoms.' Good for Bethany, I thought. 'So are you coming home for your birthday?'

'No, I'm afraid not.' I mean, why would I?

'Oh,' said Mum, 'it's just that I thought you might want to see Stevie, that's all.' That explained it. I always thought Mum was a lot fonder of Stevie than she was of me, even if she did, with gruesome tactlessness, call him 'little Stevie' to his face. I guess since I'd moved to London he hadn't been round. Maybe she missed him. 'I suppose you'll be celebrating with all your new London friends.'

'I won't be celebrating with anybody,' I snapped. 'I'll be working – in Germany, as it happens. I'm always working. You have no idea what it's like for me here.'

147

'No, Jen, I don't suppose I have. That's all right then. You just look after yourself. I'll send you a card for your birthday. Do you want HMV gift tokens as usual?'

I did see Stevie. He came up to London at the end of November. We celebrated my birthday – a week early. I took the day off. I expected Corinne to object but to my surprise she was fine about it. 'You need a break, Jen – I should have suggested it myself. We don't want you burning out.'

I was nervous about seeing Stevie. We had made up – sort of. A couple of days after I left home he texted SORRY and asked how things were going, and I texted back ME 2 and said everything was OK. Since then there had been a steady trickle of texts and emails. But there had been no face-to-face contact.

It took me ages to decide what to wear, which was ridiculous because I always wore more or less the same thing: the off-duty model uniform – jeans, T-shirt, cashmere jumper, short sharp jacket, flat boots and long skinny scarves. The days of customising charity shop finds were over. I just didn't have the time. I must have tried on four pairs of boots with about six jackets. In the end I opted for a grey wool jacket by Martin Lawn and some great Cossack vintage boots a stylist had given me on a magazine shoot in New York.

Sophie stood in my bedroom doorway, watching me, curiously, as I piled the bed with discarded clothes. She had her Blackberry in her hand – she never seemed to be without it these days. I was feeling a bit off with her because, earlier, I'd asked her who she was getting all the messages from and she'd been vague and mysterious about it. Like I even cared.

'So, this Stevie, he's your best friend?' She made it sound like a question, not a statement.

'Yes of course he is, you know he is. I've mentioned him before. God, what have I done with my skinny belt?'

'It's just that – you look like you're getting ready for a date.'

'Don't be stupid. I could never think of him that way. If you met him, you would know why.' The moment the words were out, I wanted to take them back. How horrible that sounded. It was like I was saying Stevie was repulsive – which he wasn't, not at all. But I could never think of Stevie as boyfriend material, and I knew he would never want to date me – or any girl. But I wasn't about to get into all this with Sophie.

'Do you think you'll bring him back to the flat? I mean, will I get to meet him?'

'God, Sophie, I don't know, we'll just have to see how it goes.' I really couldn't imagine why she wanted to meet him. I couldn't see them in the same room together – they belonged to such different parts of my life. I'd never been interested in meeting anybody from her past. And I ran out the door wondering if that's what I was doing: going to meet someone from my past.

* * *

Stevie was waiting for me, as arranged, outside Wagamama in Covent Garden. He was wearing blue jeans instead of his usual black, and a green parka. I didn't think I'd ever seen him in so much colour. As I crossed the road I was thinking about making some quip about his new clean-cut look but I decided against it; there was no point getting off on the wrong foot. He was reading a message on his phone so he didn't even see me until I was right in front of him.

'Nice parka,' I said.

'Yeah, thanks. Topman. Nice jacket.'

'Thanks.'

'So where's it from?'

'It was a present . . . from a publicist.' He looked at me, blankly. 'I mean it's from a designer, his publicist sent it – it's a kind of thank-you.'

'Oh. Right. Well it's great. Suits you.' We hadn't even made it inside the restaurant and already he was looking at me like I was a spoilt bitch. I really hoped he didn't notice the boots; free to me, they retailed at two thousand dollars.

'Happy birthday.' He pulled a package out of his pocket, wrapped in silvery paper, and handed it to me. 'Sorry it's early.'

'Oh, you shouldn't have, but thanks. I'll open it when we get inside.'

'Open it now,' he said, 'it's not much.' I opened it. It was a CD: the title was 'Songs for Jennifer'. 'I burned some tracks I've been listening to a lot lately. I thought you might like them. I was going to put them on a memory stick but then I thought a CD would be . . . I dunno . . . nicer.' The cover image was beautiful: pebbles on a beach in extreme close-up – or maybe they were cockles, or something else entirely – but whatever they were the mix of blues and greys really worked. I said so.

'Thanks. I had a really great camera and printer for a while and then . . .' He hesitated.

'Your dad took it back?'

'Yeah. Some things never change. Are we going inside or what? I'm starving.'

Lunch was good. Stevie loved Chinese food – even grim takeaway stuff swimming in MSG – so Wagamama hit the spot, and then some. The canteen style of the restaurant and the reasonable prices also helped him relax. I think when I suggested we meet for lunch, he thought I might drag him to Nobu or the Ivy or somewhere, but this was right up his street.

He twirled his chopsticks round some prawn noodles and grinned. Then he said, 'Omigod – is that Jake Gyllenhaal Movie Star?' I glanced around. Damn it. He was right. It was. Now he was going to think I only ever ate in celeb hangouts. Jake was hunched over a large soup bowl. No one was paying him any attention – except us. I turned back to my food. Stevie was still staring, stunned at being in the presence, a mere two tables away, of a genuine movie star. I hoped, fervently, that he wouldn't go over and ask for his autograph. I had forgotten Stevie's immunity to embarrassment. On the up side, at least he was too excited to mind my shallow, Paris Hilton lifestyle. 'The redhead he's with – oh God! – it can't be – Lindsay Lohan!'

I swung round again, appalled. Stevie was besotted with *Mean Girls*; if it was The Lohan, there would be no stopping him. The redhead had her back to us and it wasn't Lindsay Lohan's back.

'Don't be daft, Stevie, that girl's at least a size twelve.'

He smiled dreamily. 'Oh, I knew it was too good to be true. I mean – Gyllenhaal *and* The Lohan. Life isn't that kind.'

I asked him how things were at home. He dragged his gaze away from Jake and not-Lindsay.

'OK, I suppose. Bit worse than usual. *He's* never home and Mum's climbing the walls. We don't have a TV at the moment.'

'You're kidding.'

'No, he's taken them all. He left the portable in the kitchen but that's it. And the portable's not even digital.' I tried to imagine Stevie's house TV-less, and couldn't. I was going to ask him what was going on with his dad, but thought better of it. If he wanted to tell me he would. Besides, I didn't want lunch to get too heavy. We needed to have a good time today – it was important, somehow.

Stevie sighed and turned his gaze back to Jake Gyllenhaal. 'I wonder how he gets his hair to do that? God, he was brilliant in *Zodiac*. Isn't he great? Don't you think he is just so great?'

'He's eating a bowl of noodles, Stevie. I'm not really feeling the greatness right now.'

'God, sarcastic much,' muttered Stevie. Then he looked at me. 'Have you spoken to your mum lately?'

'Yeah – only the other week. Why?'

'I dunno. How did she seem?'

'Her usual cheery self.' He was right. I was sarcastic. I had to work on being less sarcastic.

'It's just that I ran into her in the mall and she seemed a bit nervy or something. It was odd.' I thought it was odd that Mum had suggested there was something up with Stevie, and now here he was hinting that something was wrong with Mum.

'If you've got something to tell me, Stevie, why don't you just tell me? I get the feeling you're keeping something from me.' I really had his attention now. 'Just – spit it out. Or at least ask me how I'm doing. Ask me something about my life.'

'Are you seeing anybody?' I wasn't expecting that.

'No. Are you?'

'I'm dating Clare Reed.'

'Very funny. If you can drag yourself away from Jake Gyllenhaal, shall we get the bill?'

17

There was no one to meet us at the airport. But that was OK. We'd both done shoots overseas before. You can't expect to have your hand held for ever. It's not like we were fourteen. I was tired from the flight but excited too: my first exotic location. Sophie had been to the island before – for a TV travel commercial, when she was five; she remembered running up and down the beach all day with two models who were pretending to be her parents.

'I'm glad it's not swimwear,' Sophie said, as we made our way to baggage reclaim to collect her case. I had my overnight bag with me.

'Yeah, me too.' I didn't fancy posing for four hours in a bikini. I'd heard things about swimwear shoots; they could attract quite a crowd.

'It's odd though, isn't it,' said Sophie, 'an eveningwear shoot on a beach? Do you think they'll put us in heels? I mean, there'll be sand – we'll sink.' Sophie didn't 'get' fashion at all; she had a very practical streak. As far as Sophie was concerned, people didn't wear five-thousand-pound-dresses on the beach so why should models. Just about everything the photographers made us do struck her as, basically, silly.

'I bet they put us in fur coats and tiaras – and then make us swim in them,' I said in my best I'm-being-totally-serious voice. Sophie, for once, didn't buy it. She giggled.

Then she said: 'Are those boys looking at us?' I turned round and, yes, they were. Or rather they were staring at Sophie. Even from a distance I was willing to bet that it was Sophie who had their eyes out on stalks; if they noticed me at all it was only because I was partially obscuring their view. We'd reached the luggage carousel. We weren't going anywhere until Sophie's case appeared. The boys could get a real eyeful.

'Oh God, one of them is coming over!' said Sophie. A boy about our age, deeply tanned and with blond sun-streaked hair, was heading straight for us.

'Excuse me, but are you a model?' He had an American accent.

Sophie was gazing at the floor; she glanced up through her hair.

'Yes, I am.'

'Cool. I thought so,' said the boy, 'you're so pretty. I told my friends you had to be a model. I'm Mark.' He put out his hand to Sophie. It was such an odd, grown-up thing to do; it made him seem really young. Sophie shook his hand, told him her name, and gave him a smile that would have melted a rock.

'This is my friend, Jen, she's a model too,' said Sophie.

'Oh right – hi, Jen,' said the boy; he didn't even glance in my direction. There was a long pause. The boy began to look a bit embarrassed. He'd started out well but he was fading fast. Sophie was looking around nervously, like she'd rather look anywhere but at the boy. The seconds dragged by. Say something Sophie, I thought, say something.

'There's my case!' She jumped and pointed. The carousel had started moving, at last; Sophie's pink case was disappearing round a corner.

'Let me,' said the boy and sped off. Two minutes later he was back; he dropped the case at her feet, looking very pleased with himself.

'Ohh . . . that's not my case,' said Sophie. It was a black Samsonite. She made it sound like the situation with the case was terribly sad, and all her fault. The boy looked mortified. 'It's OK,' said Sophie, 'let's put it back and wait for my case to come round again. I'll point it out for you.' Five minutes later they were back with Sophie's case. They looked happy – actually happy. Like they'd just got engaged or something. Suddenly it felt like they were 'Sophie and Mark' and I was the friend, tagging along. Mark threw me a bone of conversation.

'So, Jen, how long are you two on the island for?'

'Just a couple of days, we're on a shoot for a magazine.'

'That's am-az-ing,' said Mark, like it was the best news he'd heard all year. 'Hey, Sophie, maybe we could hook up tonight – if you're not working, I mean.'

'Sure, that would be nice,' said Sophie. And then, a note

of panic in her voice: 'I'm not sure what time we'll be finished, it might be late, but . . .'

'No problem. There's a club I know – Jericho's. Stays open till 3 a.m. I could pick you up any time you like. Give me your number and I'll call you later.' Sophie told him her number and he tapped it into his phone.

'Well, see you tonight, Sophie. Bye, er, Jen. Oh, if you don't mind . . .' He lifted his phone and took Sophie's picture.

'Oh!' she said. 'OK. See you later.' And he went back to his friends. There was some back-slapping and cheering. Sophie smiled and looked at her feet.

'Come on,' I said, 'let's get a cab.'

Maybe it was the contrast with the air-conditioned airport that made the heat so shocking: it was like taking your head out of a fridge and wrapping it in a boiling wet towel. After about ten seconds queueing for a taxi I told Sophie I was going back inside to get a bottle of water. She just nodded, dreamily.

It was such a relief to be in the cold, dry air. I didn't even think about Mark and his friends. I was at a kiosk, paying for the water, when I heard someone say, 'Oh man, a model! That is so freakin' cool.' I turned round and saw Mark leaning against a cigarette machine; his friends were sort of bobbing up and down. There were flashes of silver – the camera phone, being passed around.

'Yeah, she wasn't bad,' said Mark, 'not really my type though.'

'Your brother will be totally pissed,' said a gangly boy with a crew-cut. 'I mean, he made such a big friggin' deal about getting that surfer chick's number.'

'Yeah, I know,' said Mark, 'he's such a loser. Just because . . .' A tannoy announcement calling passengers to the departure gate for New York drowned out the rest. 'That's our flight,' finished Mark. 'Let's go.'

In the cab to the hotel, Sophie said, 'I think I'll wear a dress. Do you think I should wear a dress? I mean, all boys like girls in dresses, right? Or would jeans be better . . . you know, more casual.' I told her she looked great in everything. Gorgeous. I thought: I'll tell her at the hotel. I can't say it in front of the cab driver. I'll tell her later.

At the hotel there was no time to talk. Marcia, the photographer's assistant, had left a message telling us to be ready at 1 p.m., local time. That gave us five minutes to shower and change. I was drying my hair when she knocked on the door.

'Don't worry about that. You'll be getting it wet again. Just wait till you girls see the location. It'll blow your minds.'

It was forty minutes by jeep to the beach. Thank God Marcia was a good driver: it was cliff roads all the way; I didn't dare look down. There were plenty of beaches near the hotel, but this one was on the 'wrong' side of the island, ignored by tourists. Marcia parked on the road and we scrambled down a rough dirt track to the beach. Andre, the photographer, and his crew rushed over to greet us.

'Isn't it fantastic?' said Andre. He kissed us both, twice, once on each cheek. 'It's paradise after the fall. A dark heaven.' I looked around: the sand was black and there were a lot of rocks. The sea looked inky. Despite the heat, I shivered.

'Er, why is the sand black?' I asked Andre.

'It's volcanic. As in made by volcanoes like trillions of years ago.'

'It's great, really great,' I said.

An hour and a half later Sophie was lying on a rock; she was wearing a pale green dress with a long floaty train; only her shoulders and arms were bare but somehow she looked naked; a mermaid, washed up in a strange land. She lay on that rock for an hour and made it look easy, natural. When Andre asked her to get up and walk into the sea, she didn't say 'but it'll ruin the dress', as I expected her to. She just did it. And when he shouted, 'You're the sexiest girl in the world. Do something – surprise me!' she sat down in the water and laughed. It broke the intense, dreamy mood of the shoot but it was great.

Andre ran over to take some close-ups. He stood over her, water up to his knees, and told her how sexy she was, over and over again. Sophie went into a kind of trance; she offered herself up to the camera in a way I'd never seen anyone do before. The girl who didn't get fashion, who couldn't really take direction more complicated than 'give us a smile' was, for that afternoon, the best in the business.

Sophie's shoot was going so well, Andre didn't get to me for hours. I sat on a canvas chair, wrapped in a bathrobe, my make-up melting in the heat, waiting my turn. I was in no hurry. When another model is performing brilliantly on a shoot, you don't want to be the next one up. Because then you have to do something amazing to avoid looking ordinary. And it's when you're trying really hard that you come over stiff and awkward and the photographer gets tense because time is money and you're not delivering. So I sat there, watching Sophie and the sea, and hoped that Andre would forget all about me. But as the light was fading he came over to me and said, 'The sun's dropping – let's use it. It'll be the best backdrop in the world.'

I stood at the edge of the water – a blaze of colour in the sky behind me – and looked straight into the camera. He shot me for fifteen minutes and then we were done.

Back at the hotel Sophie asked if she could use the shower first. I said sure, go ahead. She came out thirty minutes later wearing a white cotton sundress and pink Haviana flip-flops. She looked, if possible, even more gorgeous than she had at the shoot.

'Is the dress OK?'

'It's perfect. Absolutely perfect.'

She sat down on the bed and picked up her phone. Then set it down again. I went into the bathroom and closed the door. I stood in the shower and watched all the gunk from the shoot – sand, body make-up, hair product – disappear down the plughole. Then I dried myself with a thick white towel and sat on the edge of the bath. I still didn't feel clean. *She wasn't bad.* He still might phone.

When I came out of the bathroom, Sophie said, 'He will phone won't he?' I said no, I didn't think he would. And then I told her everything.

'I'm so sorry, Sophie, I should have told you earlier, I don't know why I didn't. You must hate me, I'm so sorry, really I am, please . . .' She sat on the bed, completely still and quiet. Then she looked up at me.

'Let's go for a walk. I don't want to be in this room any longer,' she said.

We walked along the hotel beach. It was dark, but not so dark that you couldn't find your way. There were small groups of people sitting around beach fires. They were drinking and laughing. A couple wandered past, hand in hand; I remembered Marcia saying that this side of the island got the upmarket honeymoon crowd. The light, brittle sound of a steel band drifted down from the hotel. It made me think of an old TV ad for tropical fruit juice. I thought: she's taking it well.

'Have you ever had a boyfriend, Jen?'

There was Tommy Granger who stuck his tongue down my throat when I was twelve, which I found pretty gross. By the time I was thirteen – and might have actually appreciated a bit of lip-on-lip action – I was taller than all the boys I knew, and none of them wanted to know.

'No, not really. Not at all.'

'Me neither,' said Sophie. 'There was this boy at school I really liked. Greg. He was in the school orchestra. He asked me out. I went round to his house and we sat in his room and he played records. You know – vinyl. He hardly spoke to me all night. Then when I said it was late and I should go home he stuck his hand up my skirt. I let him. I let him do anything he wanted. I thought if I did he would like me and want to see me again. But he didn't ask me out again. He told everyone at school I was easy. Easy and boring. Lots of girls didn't like me anyway so it got pretty bad. Everybody was laughing at me and calling me names and it just went on and on, and in the end I kinda freaked out about it and got . . . ill.'

'What kind of ill?' I asked, although I was dreading what she might tell me.

'A breakdown – that's what Mum and Dad called it. I heard them talking about me one day, after I'd come back from an appointment with the psychiatrist. Mum didn't know if I would ever be "right in the head" again. She said it was just as well I could make a living out of my looks. I didn't think anything was wrong with me. It just felt like everything was bad and terrible but I was the only one who could see it.

'Anyway, I couldn't go to school for a couple of months. When I went back nobody called me names any more. They just didn't speak to me at all.'

'Oh God, Sophie, that's awful.'

'Yeah, well. After that Mum said boys were a distraction I didn't need. She said I had to think about my career. Only I'm not even much good at being a model, really. I'm not like you, Jen. So a lot of the time, I just feel like I'm letting my mum – everybody – down. I just feel so lonely.'

'Oh Soph, Soph . . .' She started to cry. It wasn't the sort of crying you would expect from a girl who looked like Sophie. It sounded like an animal with its leg in a trap. I looked around but there was no one to see her or hear her; we'd been walking for half an hour; this end of the beach was deserted. I wished Corinne was here, or Madja, or even my mum. Anybody – any adult who could tell me what to do, who could make it better for Sophie. I tried telling her that Mark and Greg were idiots, nasty, no-mark knob-heads. She laughed when I said 'knob-head'. I put my arm round her waist, the way Stevie used to do for me, and told her she was too good for those stupid boys. Too good, and far too pretty.

'But what's the point, Jen, of being this pretty when no one wants you? I know I look OK. I mean people are really keen at first and then they just . . . go off me. So it must be me that's the problem. It must be what's on the inside that isn't good enough.'

'You *are* good enough, Sophie – of course you're good enough! You're brilliant.' But I didn't know how to convince her, or what else to say.

* * *

Next day's shoot went badly for Sophie. She couldn't seem to do anything right. She moved awkwardly in the clothes, and had one look on her face – a sort of blank indifference. It wasn't the look Andre wanted.

'Are we boring you, Sophie?' he said, finally losing his temper. 'You don't seem to be with us, dear. Where is the girl from yesterday? Can we have her back please?' But that girl was gone for good.

18

Two days after we got back from the island shoot, Corinne called me into her office. We talked about some castings I had scheduled for next week, and the possibility of a trip to Tokyo to do a clothing catalogue. Corinne said the Tokyo trip wouldn't do anything for my profile – the catalogue would only be seen in Japan – but it would be 'obscenely well paid'.

I was trying to imagine what an obscene amount of money might be, when she said, 'So, Jen, what happened on the island? I spoke to Andre. He said you were great, from start to finish, a total pro.' I tried to smile, look happy. 'But something was up with Sophie. Day one of the shoot she was the star – day two, totally out of it. A "zombie" to use Andre's expression.'

'Why don't you ask Sophie?'

'If I ask Sophie she will say sorry for an hour and then cry. And I still won't know what happened. I'm asking you. You're the responsible one.' Was I? Why? Sophie was the same age as me, and far more experienced as a model. Corinne got out of her chair and came round to my side of the desk. She leaned against the desk and looked down at me. I was sitting in the giant purple chair and for the first time ever it wasn't comfortable.

'Look, you two are friends I know, and I respect that. I'm not asking you to tell tales or get Sophie into trouble. And I'm sure that whatever happened, it wasn't your fault. But try to see it from my point of view. I have to keep an eye out for you girls. If there's a problem I can't just look the other way. When a girl performs really well one day and then bombs out the next, it raises all sorts of red flags. Did Sophie take something? Is she using?'

'Using?'

'Drugs, Jen, is Sophie using drugs?' This seemed so ridiculous that, for a second, I was relieved. 'I mean, I'm a realist. I know you girls work long hours and spend a lot of time away from home. I know you get offered stuff – pills to wake you up or calm you down, or just take the edge off things.'

'These pills, they sound great. Where can I get some?' I was trying to lighten the mood, maybe even make her laugh, but it just came out sounding snide and defensive.

'This isn't funny, Jen. I need to know.' She didn't sound angry, or even annoyed. Just tried that she had to have this conversation, and bored by my resistance.

'It's not drugs. Honest. It was nothing like that.'

'OK, that's good. So, what was it? Because whatever it was, I'd like to help Sophie. You do want me to help her, don't you?'

I told Corinne; how could I not? But it all sounded really juvenile and lame: some guy chats up Sophie for ten minutes and then he doesn't phone and she's heartbroken. At the time it felt like so much more than that, but I couldn't explain why. I gave Corinne the bare bones of what had happened and she didn't ask for anything else.

When I was finished, she said, 'Poor Sophie, she doesn't have the emotional maturity to handle rejection. It must have been upsetting for her.' It was, I said, it really was – she dressed up for him and waited all night for him at the hotel, and he was a total pig. Corinne smiled sympathetically as I babbled, and then said, 'But you know, something that small should never affect work. The shoot cost the client thousands. Andre is a top photographer – he is used to working with the best. Fortunately he got some great shots, but if it had gone the other way it would have damaged not just Sophie's reputation, but the agency's.'

Maybe it was all my fault, I thought. Maybe if I'd said the right things to Sophie that night on the beach, she wouldn't still have been upset the next day. I started to apologise to Corinne but the words stuck in my throat; I wished she wouldn't look at me like that. Suddenly, I didn't feel at all apologetic.

'I don't know why you're telling me all this – I didn't do anything. Why don't you tell it to Sophie?'

'Oh, I will, Jen, I will.'

* * *

When I finally got out of Corinne's office it was 3 p.m. and there was no time to think. I was due at a magazine shoot on the other side of town in forty-five minutes. I ran to the tube, glad of the cold winter air against my cheeks, and, without even having to check my tube map, made it to the shoot with ten minutes to spare.

It was a simple, fun shoot and I loved it. There were six models – three girls and three boys – and all we had to do was jump up and down in front of a white backdrop wearing neon-bright clothes. For most of the shoot I wore an orange miniskirt, so short you could see my bum cheeks, and a lime green strapless top that barely covered my breasts. The clothes were ugly – there was nothing sexy about them at all. We must have looked like long, thin Teletubbies. It was like being a kid again. I jumped and jumped and jumped.

I got back to the flat at about 2 a.m.; I'd been to a club with some models from the shoot. I thought there was no risk of me running into Sophie – she usually went to bed about 10.30 with a milky drink. But she was up, sitting in the living room, on her own, in the dark.

'You told her. About Mark. You told Corinne.' There was an anger in her voice that I'd never heard before; it was unnerving. I couldn't have this conversation in the dark. I sat down on the sofa – Sophie was in the armchair opposite – and switched on a table lamp.

'I had to, Sophie – she thought you were on drugs. What was I supposed to do?'

'You were supposed to keep it to yourself. You were supposed to be my friend.'

'God, Sophie, it's late, I'm knackered, can we do this in the morning?'

'You told her. I trusted you – *and you told her.*' Sophie, shouting, set something off in me. If she had sat there whispering her misery at me I might have taken it; I might have apologised all night. But if she was strong enough to shout at me, then, somehow, it was OK for me to throw it right back at her.

'Enough! I've had it! Corinne going on at me like I'm your bloody keeper, and now you sitting here making a big bloody drama out of something that is not my fault! I had to tell Corinne – she heard you acted like a zombie at the shoot. I had to convince her you weren't a junkie.'

'You knew how I felt about Mark . . .'

'Oh forget Mark, you knew him for fifteen minutes, get over it. You know what your problem is, Sophie? *You don't have the emotional maturity to deal with rejection.*' I was going to take it back, I swear I was, but suddenly the main light came on.

'Jeez, could you two keep the bloody noise down, I have a 6 a.m. call . . .'

I glared at Natalie, who'd appeared at the door, and stomped off to bed. I fell asleep, instantly, knowing that me and Sophie, our friendship, was over.

But a few hours later Sophie shook me awake. The room was never really dark because of the streetlights outside, so I could see her face, quite clearly, close to mine. She'd been crying.

'Don't be angry with me, Jen, please don't, I can't bear it. I'm sorry, I'm sorry. I know I'm pathetic and get upset about nothing, I know . . .' I sat up and put my arms round her; she was freezing. Everything I'd said to her, all the vile, cruel things, came back in a rush. I could have drowned in shame.

'You're not pathetic, Sophie, you had every right to be upset about what Mark did. It was horrible. Corinne doesn't know, she wasn't there. And I'm the stupid one – I shouldn't have said all that stuff about emotional maturity – I don't even know what it means. It was just something mean to say, cos I was tired and pissed off. And I'm so sorry, Sophie, I'm sorry, I'm sorry, I'm sorry . . .' And then we were both crying, and Sophie got into my bed and I warmed her feet with mine and we fell asleep.

19

I was packing for Tokyo when Corinne called me. I thought something was wrong for a moment, her voice sounded so tight and strained. Then I realised: she was excited.

'Forget Tokyo. You've got the Elegance job. They need you in Paris – tomorrow.'

I was confused. Corinne, who always put the client first, had pulled me out of the catalogue job in Tokyo at the last moment. It didn't make sense. The client would be furious. And what about the 'obscene amounts of money' I'd be losing?

She laughed when I said this in so many words. 'Oh Jen – you really have no idea what this means, do you? Elegance are the second biggest premium cosmetics firm in the world. And you're going to be their house model – the face of the brand. This is huge. It catapults you into the big league.'

I sat down on my bed and stared at a pair of knickers drying over a radiator. I could hear Sophie in the next room, her voice harsher than normal, practising her German.

'Do you think the weather will be the same in Paris as in Tokyo?' I asked. 'Only I've already packed for Tokyo . . .'

Corinne said she was sending round an assistant who would do my packing for me. She would take care of all the travel arrangements, accompany me to Paris and make sure I had everything I needed during the shoot. I thought: I'm going to be stuck with a complete stranger – what if we don't get on?

'Jen – don't you want to know how much Elegance will be paying you?'

'Yeah, I suppose so. Yes of course I do. How much?'

She told me.

'Can you just repeat that?' I asked, shocked. She gave me the figure again. It was a frightening amount of money. 'Oh God,' I said. 'Oh God!'

Corinne laughed, again. I had no idea why she was finding this conversation so funny.

'Congratulations Jen. You're a millionaire.'

On the Eurostar to Paris my assistant, Traci, sat in economy while I lorded it in first class. I only noticed our tickets were different when we were on the platform at Waterloo, about to board the train. I was mortified. I tried to swap tickets with her, but she wasn't having it.

'If the agency found out I'd probably get the sack. This is how it is – you're the talent, I'm the assistant. I love my job and I'm going to Paris to stay in a five-star hotel. It ain't too shabby. You'll get used to having a servant, trust me. In a day or two you'll probably be throwing your phone at me.'

'Oh God, I won't! Honest, I could never . . .'

'I'm kidding. Here . . .' she pushed a copy of French *Vogue* into my hands, 'look at this on the train. It's filled with adverts from the current Elegance campaign. You can see the girl you're replacing. She's history.'

Traci was a blast. She reminded me a lot of Marcia from the island shoot: down to earth, upbeat and capable. They even looked alike – the same hazel eyes and stocky build. I asked her if she knew Marcia.

' 'Fraid so. She's my sister. It's kind of a family business. We live to serve the beautiful. Now will you get your skinny rump on that train?' There was clearly no possibility of me or anybody else bossing Traci around. I stopped arguing and got on the train.

First class was filled, unsurprisingly, with businessmen and businesswomen. Everyone was suited and booted and older than me. I wondered if they wondered what I was doing travelling first class. I must have looked like a gap year student in my usual skinny jeans and jumper combo. Or maybe not. The jeans were the latest designer brand to hit New York – they weren't even available in Harvey Nichols until next month – and the jumper was the finest, softest cashmere. It took a lot of money to look this casual. Maybe they thought I was a millionaire's daughter, off on a trip to visit Daddy. What a joke. The suits tapped at their laptops. I opened my magazine.

The 'girl' I was replacing was thirty-two-year-old A-list actress Grace Watts. The woman had two Oscars. She was, of course, terribly beautiful, but had made her name playing ugly in gritty parts involving sexual humiliation or terminal illness. (Her most successful role had been as a cancer patient who gets gang-raped by escaped convicts. The Academy had virtually thrown the Oscar at her.)

I looked at her, spread seductively over two pages, her violet eyes inviting the viewer to love her, die for her. And they were binning Grace Watts for *me* – a seventeen-year - old who had done nothing but walk down a few runways, and pose for some pictures. It was a strange business.

The train emerged from the tunnel. We were in France. Maybe it was my imagination but even the trees looked French – slender, refined. I thought back to the dinner I had had a couple of weeks back with the people from Elegance.

I hadn't even realised it at the time but the dinner was a casting. Corinne had been vague about why she wanted me to go: 'They're good contacts,' she'd said, 'they might come in handy in the future.' I knew something was up when she couriered round a cream Chloé shift dress, along with a pair of Christian Louboutin slingbacks. Her note read: 'No red lipstick. Keep your face bare.'

She didn't tell me how important the meeting was, I think, because she couldn't risk me being nervous. She was giving the client what they wanted: a fresh, natural girl. A girl who didn't try too hard.

To my surprise it was Madja, not Corinne, who was waiting for me at the restaurant. She was wearing a hat which appeared to have been made out of stuffed birds; several sets of glass eyes stared blankly. It suited her. She stood on her tiptoes and kissed me; a feather tickled my cheek.

'I've known the creative director at Elegance since the late seventies,' said Madja, as she led me to our table. 'Henri is a lovely boy – well he's all grown up now. Not a bit grand. He'll love you.'

I don't know if the creative director of Elegance 'loved' me, exactly, but he watched me, all through dinner. There was nothing sinister or oppressive about it: it was a calm, cool assessment. Elegance's marketing director, a tiny brunette in a Chanel suit, kept up a stream of small talk. She made everything sound amusing and of equal importance. Madja pulled me into the conversation occasionally. Several times she patted me on the hand, as though as I was a child who she was rather fond of.

At the end of the dinner, Madja said, 'So, tell me, Henri, has your trip to London been worthwhile?'

'I think so, yes. Most girls today – the T-shirt generation – are too knowing, too casual. Mademoiselle Jones is different – you did not exaggerate. She has innocence and sophistication. I have enjoyed meeting her.' I'm right here, I thought, I'm sitting right here.

The last thing Madja said to me, before she put me in a taxi, was: 'Be a good girl and hang that dress up tonight. We have to send it back to Chloé in the morning. I'll have a word with the Louboutin people. Maybe you can keep the shoes. You deserve them. You did very well.' I didn't think I had done anything at all.

I packed the shoes and brought them with me to Paris. Since they had helped get me the Elegance job, I thought they might bring me luck on the shoot. As it turned out, I needed all the luck I could get.

The atmosphere on the set was quieter and more serious than usual. There were occasional visitors, middle-aged suits ('the money men' Traci called them) who stood discreetly at the back of the studio. I recognised Henri among them, but he didn't come over or attempt to attract my attention.

The photographer, who everyone addressed as 'Madame', asked me to empty my head of all distractions. She wanted me to be 'clean and pure – like a river'. I thought of nothing at all. Madame took so many close-ups my eyes watered from the effort of not blinking, but it was easier than most shoots. A good photographer makes it easy because they know exactly what they want. Madame was very good. There were no gimmicks: no posing in tanks of water, or hanging from a trapeze, or pretending to be in love with another model. There was no story to this campaign and hardly any body: it was just a face – my face.

At 4.30 p.m. on the third and final day, Madame handed the camera to her assistant, kissed me on the forehead, and said, 'Merci, Jennifer.' Everyone applauded. The chief make-up artist was so overcome with emotion, he started to cry. I gathered the shoot had been a success. It was over.

* * *

At 6p.m. I was lying in a bath in my suite at the Hotel Costes. Traci was downstairs in the bar, people-watching. (Her sister had spotted Nicole Kidman and her husband in the Costes bar a month ago. Determined to top this, Traci was hoping for Brangelina. 'They're in Paris – Brad's filming. Where else would they stay but Costes?')

We were booked on the 8 p.m. train back to London.

My phone rang. I let it ring. I had a feeling it was Corinne. I had already spoken to a triumphant Madja ('Henri said you were perfection, dearie. Perfection!') and was feeling light-headed with all the praise. If I got any more compliments today my head might explode. Much safer to lie here in the perfumed water. I thought: how can a bathroom be this beautiful? Even the toilet was beautiful.

My phone rang again. And again. I was already clambering out of the bath when I heard a frantic knocking and Traci's voice, just audible from the corridor outside my room. 'Jen! Answer your phone. Corinne needs to speak to you. It's urgent!' I ran, naked, to the bed and grabbed my phone out of my jeans pocket. Traci was still banging on the door. I shouted for her to be quiet.

'Corinne – what's wrong?'

'Your mother has been arrested for shoplifting. She stole some cosmetics – Elegance cosmetics. It's very embarrassing for the brand. They may drop you.'

'I don't understand.'

'There's a morals clause in the contract.' Corinne sounded unnaturally calm. She was very angry. 'If you or anyone connected to you brings the brand into disrepute they can tear it up. You're so level-headed – no drugs or men – I never thought . . . There'll be a cancellation fee but it's nothing, nothing compared to the value of the contract. It's a disaster.'

'Oh God.'

'You've got to stay where you are. I'm coming out to Paris tonight, with Madja. If we can talk to the Elegance people before the story reaches the media then we might be able to calm them down – convince them we can spin it, get some sympathetic coverage. "Teen model escapes difficult background to land fairytale contract." They just might buy it. Henri adored you. You have to see him – convince him you are worth the trouble. I'll set up a meeting.'

I grabbed a towel, wrapped it round me, sat down on the bed.

'I don't understand how my mum can have been arrested for shoplifting. She's not a thief. Is she all right? *Is my mum all right?*' There was a long pause.

'She phoned me herself to tell me what had happened. She thought it might cause trouble for you. She's fine. Of course you're concerned – we all are – but there's nothing you can do for your mum. You need to concentrate on the Elegance situation.'

I walked over to the door and let in a white-faced Traci. She sat on the edge of bed, and waited. As soon as I was off the phone she would talk to me, calm me down, pick out the clothes I should wear for my meeting with Henri.

'No.' I was surprised at how steady my voice sounded. I wasn't going to cry or shout, after all.

'What do you mean?' said Corinne.

'You and Madja can look after the Elegance situation. I'm going home. My mum needs me.'

Mum was her usual self. She poured me a cup of tea and asked me if I wanted a biscuit; there were some chocolate HobNobs in the cupboard.

'It's a mistake, isn't it, Mum?'

She shook her head. 'Come upstairs. I've got something to show you.'

Bewildered, I followed her to her bedroom. She pulled a suitcase out from under the bed, and opened it. It was filled with clothes I didn't recognise – clothes I had never seen her wear. I picked up a blouse: it was a size fourteen. My mum is a size eight. The security tag was still attached to the sleeve.

'The alarm doesn't go off all the time, despite the tags. Some shops are easy – you can just walk out. But I've had to run for it a couple of times. I had a bad scare, a while back, in Next. Bumped into Stevie straight afterwards. I don't know what he must have thought of me. I was in a right state. Lately I've been taking a pair of scissors with me. Look –' She handed me a skirt: there was a large hole in the waistband, where the tag must have been.

That's when I started to cry.

* * *

Mum had been stealing from shops since I was a baby.

'It started after your father left us. Just small things – a lipstick from the chemist or a pair of tights. The first time it happened I couldn't believe what I'd done. I was so ashamed. But gradually . . . I started taking bigger items – tops and bottoms, even coats. Sometimes I can go for months without lifting a thing and then I get down or upset about something and it all starts up again.

'I know it doesn't make sense, but when I take something it makes me feel better – elated. By the time I get home, I'm so disgusted with myself I feel worse than ever.

'Anyway, last week I went to that big new department store in the mall to buy your Aunt Pat some perfume for her birthday, and they had this big Elegance promotion on. There were big pictures everywhere of that actress who does the adverts for them. And I knew that was going to be you soon. I got to thinking about how quiet the house is without you, and then, suddenly, there was all this stuff in my bag. I don't even remember taking it. The security guard must have been standing next to me. I've been so stupid.'

We were both sitting on the bedroom floor. Mum had her arms folded tight across her stomach. I closed the suitcase and pushed it back under the bed. I couldn't bear to look at it any more. I put my arms round her.

'It's going to be OK, Mum. It will. I'll get you a good lawyer – the best. I can afford it. Madja will know who to go to, she knows everyone.'

Mum gently pushed me away.

'No, Jen, I don't need a fancy lawyer. I'd rather be in prison than go on this way. And anyway, I don't want you spending your money on me. I've probably lost you the Elegance job. Corinne was very upset when I told her. I'm sorry.'

'Forget about the money. I'm going to get you a decent lawyer. Let's not even argue about that. And you're not going to prison.' As I said this, I hoped desperately that it was true. 'You're not a criminal. You just need some help – counselling, someone to work out why you do this and help you to stop.'

Mum took a deep breath and let it out slowly. I could see her thinking, really thinking, about what I'd said.

'You've grown up a lot, Jen.' I didn't reply; I wasn't interested in talking about me. 'I have tried, you know, to sort myself out. I've made lots of appointments at the GP surgery. But when I see the doctor, I just can't get the words out. Last time I ended up telling him I thought I had a urinary tract infection. I came out with a prescription for antibiotics.'

'I'll go with you, OK? We'll talk to the doctor together, explain what's been happening, and he'll get you some help. Please, Mum – please say you'll go.'

'All right then. If you think it will help . . .'

'It will, I know it will.'

I hugged her, and this time she didn't pull away.

20

You would think that would be enough for one week, wouldn't you? The biggest contract of my career hanging in the balance, my mum exposed as a compulsive shoplifter. But no. Trouble and misery hadn't finished with me yet. There was more to come.

Stevie had texted me a lot when I was in Paris. The texts were annoyingly mysterious: (CALL ME WHEN YOU CAN. ARE YOU FREE TO TALK?) That kind of thing. I replied, just once, to tell him I was very busy and I'd call him when I got back to London. The truth is I didn't want to know what was up. I couldn't risk getting involved in some crisis in case it rattled me and affected my performance on the Elegance shoot. So I ignored the texts and I kept my focus on work. Corinne had taught me well.

When the story about Mum's arrest hit the papers, Stevie didn't text to ask how she was. That surprised me. In fact, since I had got back from Paris, it had all gone quiet on the Stevie front. I still didn't pick up the phone. Being a supportive daughter was a stretch; maybe I didn't have it in me to be a good friend too.

It was my cousin Bethany who said I should go round and see him. 'I think the family's going through a pretty bad time. Something to do with his dad, I heard. I thought you'd want to know.'

I knocked on the front door. It swung open. I went inside. There was no carpet in the hall or on the stairs and it was very cold, as though the heating hadn't been on for days. I tried to walk quietly. I went into the living room and it had been stripped bare. There wasn't even a light bulb hanging. I shivered.

People move house, I told myself, it's no big deal. All their furniture would be in the new house. Stevie might be unpacking right now.

I turned to go – I didn't want to be caught snooping when the new owners turned up – and then a noise, from upstairs, stopped me. I went to the bottom of the stairs and listened. Nothing. But I had to be sure.

I walked up the stairs and went straight to Stevie's room. I paused outside the door, listening. There was no sound. I had been in that room a thousand times; part of my childhood belonged there. I opened the door and saw Stevie, lying on a bare mattress on the floor, and in his arms – a fair-haired girl. The girl opened her eyes and looked at me: Clare Reed. She shook Stevie awake: 'Look, Stevie, look who's here.' Look who's here.

Stevie twisted round: 'You.' I turned and ran. If I hadn't

stumbled on the stairs I might have made it out of the house. But he was faster, and sure-footed. He caught up with me in the hall, grabbed my arm, pulled me back.

'What the hell are you doing here?'

'What am I doing? What the hell are you doing with Clare Reed?'

'She's my girlfriend. I told you, but you thought I was joking. *You thought I was such a loser it didn't even occur to you it could be true.*' He was shaking with rage. If I hadn't been so angry myself, I might have been scared.

'Clare? But you're . . .'

'What? Gay? That's what you've always assumed isn't it?'

'You should have told me.' I felt weak, defeated.

'You should have asked.'

I leaned against the wall and closed my eyes. All those times at school – Clare and Louise asking if me and Stevie were going to a party, making the effort to be friends, being nice, being nice. But not because they pitied me. Being nice because Clare wanted Stevie and I was his best friend. I'd been wrong about the twins, I'd been wrong about everything.

'I can't take this, I've got enough to deal with.' I reached for the door, opened it an inch or two. Stevie slammed it shut.

'Yeah, I heard. Your mum's a thief. Well guess what? So is my dad. Only he hasn't been robbing lipsticks – he's big time. And he's going to jail for a long, long time, and everything we own has been repossessed. We've lost

184

everything. *Look at this place.* Weren't you even going to ask?'

I couldn't speak. Clare's voice, full of concern, full of love, drifted down the stairs: 'Don't, Stevie, don't. It's Jen – she's still your friend. Please – stop.'

But Stevie couldn't stop. We had gone too far, the two of us, and all of Clare's love and gentleness could not prevent us from reaching our bitter end. I looked at him and I felt no pity.

'I don't know you. And I don't want to know you.' Stevie opened the door. 'Get out, Jen. You're dead to me now.' I stepped out into the winter sunlight and the door shut behind me.

You could say I got lucky. The department store prosecuted Mum but she got off with a suspended sentence. Corinne released a statement to the press. The last paragraph read:

Psychological problems led to the incident which Mrs Jones deeply regrets. She is now receiving the counselling she needs to address her behaviour and move forward. Jennifer Jones wishes to thank the senior management and staff at Elegance Cosmetics for their continuing support at this difficult time. She will be at Bloomingdale's in New York City on May 23 at 1 p.m. for the launch of Elegance's superb new fragrance, 'Captive'.

Stevie's dad got sent down for five years. Mum sent me a cutting from the local paper. I read it quickly and then tore it up, and threw the pieces away.

I was working so hard I didn't have time for regrets – at least, not during the day. Despite how tired I was, I had trouble sleeping. I got used to waking up in the night, my mind racing with dreams. There were a lot of dreams about Stevie; sometimes we were kids again, playing, having fun; and then I'd remember. As soon as I remembered we weren't friends any more I would put the light on, because I couldn't bear to cry in the dark. In the morning I got up and went to work and it was all right. I didn't think about him when I was working.

Being Elegance's house model turned out to involve a lot more than the odd photo shoot. I was contractually obliged to attend product launches and promotional events all over the word.

I was photographed spraying myself with 'Captive' in Sydney, Moscow, Bangkok and Cape Town. Elegance used me as a battering ram to open new markets in countries which had never before felt the need for a eighty dollar bottle of scent. Ditching an Oscar-winning actress for a seventeen-year-old virtual unknown guaranteed a healthy level of publicity for the brand. But the human interest story of Mum's arrest and trial pushed the media interest off the scale. When I cried on Japanese television the clip made the top ten on YouTube. Everyone blamed the interviewer for grilling me on my mother's 'shame'. In fact, I was just jet-lagged and coming down with flu. But the truth did not make a good story, so it wasn't believed.

After the Japanese sob-fest Corinne made me take a week off. I spent most of it sleeping. She sent me to a dietician who prescribed an immune-system-boosting diet full of oily fish, green leafy vegetables and a really incredible amount of blueberries. I travelled everywhere with Traci and a changing cast of personal trainers. The trainers devised work-out routines which could fit into any hotel room. (Elegance didn't want me papped looking sweaty and crap in a gym.) I wasn't just thin any more: I was toned.

An Elegance dermatologist was on call twenty-four hours a day to ensure the face of the brand was never marred by spots or dry patches. I was exfoliated, scrubbed and moisturised until my skin glowed. I had never looked better.

I was miserable.

Corinne told me not to get complacent.

'You're not at the top yet, Jen. There is another tier of success, just above you. If you carry on working this hard I'm sure you can make it. The era of top models being tied exclusively to one brand is over. You can broaden your range by working for different brands that appeal to different markets. Elegance is just the beginning. If we get it right then you will become the brand.'

She said this to me in a hotel suite. It was 8 a.m., local time. My trainer was hovering in the background, ready to coach me through my first one hundred abdominal crunches of the day. I don't remember which country I was in – after three capital cities in one day in June, I stopped noticing. But I remember what she said, so clearly, every word of it. *If we get it right then you will become the brand.* I thought: I don't want to be a brand; I'm a model – a girl who is photographed for a living. That's all. It should be simple. It should be easier than this.

'Corinne – I want to do Paris Fashion Week, in September.'

'Why? There's no need. Sure the Elegance campaign will be slowing down by then but there are plenty of other big names dying to sign you.'

'I don't care. I need a break.' I actually saw doing the shows as a break. 'Call it back to basics. I'm serious, Corinne.'

'Well, if you're sure.' She tore off a piece of croissant. I ate a spoonful of bio-yoghurt and blueberries. She didn't like it, I could tell, but she wasn't going to push the point. Ever since I'd left Paris to be with my mum, Corinne had been careful not to get on my wrong side. She'd flown thousands of miles to be with me now because I had started to complain about my schedule. It was in everybody's interests to keep me sweet. 'I suppose if you go to Paris, Madja will be pleased at any rate. You know how old-fashioned she is about the shows. She still thinks they matter. And you're her favourite runway girl.'

'Am I? I thought that was Francine.'

'No, it's you. At least it has been since Francine threw

away her career to raise a bunch of brats.' Corinne did not think models had any business becoming mothers.

'There's something else,' I said.

'What?' Corinne looked suspicious.

'Give Traci a holiday – she's earned it. I won't need an assistant at the shows. I know the ropes. I want to go to Paris with Sophie. And Bella too, if we can lure her out of Cornwall. I hardly ever see them any more.'

'Sophie? Are you sure? Do you think she's up to it? We've been keeping her away from the shows. Her walk has never been that great, you know.'

'Yes of course she's up to it. You always underestimate her. I'm going to Paris and I'm taking Sophie with me. If we can get Bella to come too, then Giovanni can send the three of us down the runway again. I heard he's showing in Paris this season. The press will love it.'

'Actually, you're right – that could work.' She looked impressed. 'You've come a long way, Jen.' I didn't answer. I wasn't particularly interested in Corinne's thoughts on my development. 'OK, I'll talk to Bella – she was going to skip Paris but if she only has to do Giovanni's show, she'll make the effort, for once.'

'And Sophie?'

'Oh, Sophie will go wherever we send her.'

If it hadn't been for me, Sophie would have been safe in London. She would never have met Guido again.

21

'Jen, Sophie – this is my mother, Caroline. Say hello to my friends, Mummy, and try not to frighten them.'

Bella's mother shook hands, first with Sophie and then with me. Her handshake was firm, definite. I had expected a posh woman of a certain age, typically English, a keen gardener, dressed for comfort. But the woman in front of me was a lesson in style.

She was wearing couture Chanel as though she never wore anything else. Her dark shoulder-length hair was pushed back from her face, and her make-up was so expertly applied I could not be sure that she was wearing any. A gold wedding band was her only jewellery. Mrs Devine gave the impression of someone who had nothing to hide, someone who made no effort to please. I had been scraping my make-up off – Giovanni's Paris show had just finished – but I stopped as soon as Mrs Devine turned up. Even before she spoke, she had my full attention.

'Did you enjoy the show?' I asked her.

'Not really, no. You girls were charming, of course,' said Mrs Devine, 'but the concept' – her forehead creased with a barely perceptible frown – 'was ridiculous. So typical of Giovanni.'

Giovanni had jumped at the chance to repeat his 'English Family' triumph, but unfortunately his inspiration for this season's collection was global warming and the melting of the ice caps. So he had sent us down the runway as a family of Eskimos.

'Oh, it could have been worse,' laughed Bella, 'he could have made us dress up as polar bears.' She stepped out of her faux-fur-trimmed trouser suit and pulled on a pair of jeans and a T-shirt. 'Why on earth did you come?' she asked her mother. 'You never come to the shows and you can't stand Giovanni.'

'I came to keep an eye on you, Bella. I don't want you socialising with that man again.'

Bella rolled her eyes. 'God, it was one party! I hardly set eyes on him and, anyway, he's completely harmless.'

'Giovanni may be, yes, but his friends are appalling.'

'Caroline! There you are.' It was Bella's father. The button was still missing from his coat. 'There's someone here you just have to meet – Guy Willis, I went to school with him. His daughter is here – she's a model too, can you believe it?'

'Daddy, can't you leave Mummy alone for five minutes?' said Bella. 'You're always dragging her off to meet your business contacts.'

Mr Devine looked like he was about to protest, but his wife cut him off.

'Of course I'll meet the man. Come on, Charles – the girls need to get changed.' I was grateful to her – Sophie and I were burning up in our Eskimo outfits. As she led him away, Mrs Devine looked over her shoulder and said, 'You better be here when we get back. I'm serious, Bella.'

'She's wonderful, isn't she?' said Bella as her parents walked away.

'Yes,' I said, truthfully, 'she really is.'

Bella's parents had been gone less than five minutes when Giovanni appeared with about six or seven hangers-on. He was about to say something to Bella, when a tall dark-haired man cut through the crowd and embraced him. It was Guido – the man who had kissed Sophie at Giovanni's party in Milan. I glanced at Sophie to see how she would react. She went a bit pink but she didn't look surprised. The two men's embrace lasted only a few seconds; when it was over Guido stepped back into the crowd.

'Ah, Bella, have I missed your mother? Has she left already?' said Giovanni.

'I think she might have,' said Bella.

Giovanni looked heartbroken. 'What a pity. I was so hoping to see her. It's been such a long time. I put your parents in the front row, of course. Did your mother like the show?'

'She loved it,' said Bella, coldly.

Giovanni smiled. 'Yes, everyone is being so kind . . .' and then an assistant arrived and dragged him off. The crowd went with him – only Guido remained. He walked straight over to Sophie and took her hand. I don't know what he said to Sophie – he spoke in Italian – but it made her face light up. If Sophie hadn't been blushing they might have passed for old friends. If he hadn't been looking at her the way he was, he might have been mistaken for her uncle. Bella looked at me, amazed. 'Who is the creepy old guy?' she whispered. I shrugged. I didn't really know what to say, and anyway, there was no opportunity to tell her anything because her mobile rang; she fished it out of her bag. 'Hugo – you're breaking up!' she screeched above the din of a fashion show packing up and moving on. 'I'm going outside. The reception is rubbish here. I said *outside*!' She grabbed her bag and hurried off.

The party was the beginning, I thought, all that time ago in Milan. There have been emails, texts – something to make Sophie act now as if she knows Guido. She thinks she knows him.

Sophie introduced me to him. He looked at me the way he had looked at me at the party: an instant assessment and dismissal. Close up, Guido was almost too handsome. He had had some work done, perhaps even a face-lift. His skin was perfectly smooth but not young. In Milan I had thought he might be thirty-five, now I realised he was at least ten years older.

When he had finished being barely polite to me he turned the full force of his attention back on Sophie. He reached out and tucked a strand of hair behind her ear. I wanted to hit him. But Sophie appeared happy, excited, in his company. Then he leaned in close, whispered in her ear – and kissed her on the mouth. It was a longer kiss than the one I had witnessed in Milan. I looked away – and saw Mrs Devine, just visible in a crowd, making her way towards us. I remembered, suddenly, her calling Giovanni's friends 'appalling'. When I looked back to see if Guido had noticed her, he was gone. There was no time to have it out properly with Sophie – Bella's mother was almost within earshot – but I couldn't let it go either.

'Sophie – have you kept in touch with him since Milan?'

'So what if I have?' she said. 'I'm allowed to have my own friends, aren't I?'

'Friends? Are you kidding me? He was all over you like a rash and he's twice your age. It's creepy.'

'Guido is *nice* – he makes me feel *wonderful*.'

'*You are off your head!*' I hissed. Sophie opened her mouth to reply and then shut it again. I glanced round: Mrs Devine. She either hadn't heard, or wasn't interested in, our teenage spat.

'Where's Bella?' she asked me.

'Outside, on her mobile, talking to Hugo. The signal in here is—'

'Well, that's all right. Shall we go outside and join her? Colin is bringing the car round.'

I picked up my bag and pulled on my jacket, but Sophie hung back.

Mrs Devine gave her an enquiring look. She got to her feet.

'Oh, sorry. Yes, I'm coming.'

Outside on the street Mrs Devine waited patiently in the car while Bella paced up and down the pavement, yakking to Hugo. I had a feeling she approved of Hugo. Colin was in the driver's seat, reading a paper. Sophie was sat beside me, staring dreamily out of the car window. There was no sign of Mr Devine.

'I've been impressed by your work for Elegance, Jennifer,' said Mrs Devine, clicking her seatbelt into place. 'The simplicity in those first photographs was so effective. It reminded me a little of a campaign I worked on in the 1980s for Armani.' I tried to hide my surprise. Bella had mentioned that her mother 'did a bit of modelling in the eighties'; she hadn't said she had worked for big designers. But it made perfect sense. Mrs Devine had the kind of poise that only the best models have; I'd seen it in Erin O'Connor and Giselle.

'Thanks . . .' the car door opened and Bella clambered inside, 'I've been very lucky,' I said.

'How have you been lucky, Jen?' Bella slammed the door shut.

'Er, the Elegance campaign, you know. Your mum was just . . . being nice about it.'

'Really? She's never says anything nice about my career – do you, Mummy? When I said I was going to give modelling a go, you practically tied me to a chair.'

'But I needn't have worried, Bella. You are so lazy you will probably have retired by the time you're twenty. The

195

fashion business has no chance of getting its hooks into you – not unless it relocates to Cornwall.'

'Oh I won't stick it out till I'm twenty,' said Bella, who didn't seem to feel the sting in her mother's words, 'that's two years' away. Hugo and I will be running the farm on his father's estate by then. We're making plans. Organic – that's where the money is. I'm not lazy when it's something I care about. Or not quite so lazy, anyway.' And mother and daughter smiled at each other.

I realised with a jolt that Bella and Hugo were practically engaged. Bella had her whole life mapped out.

She was one of the few models I knew who even had a boyfriend. I remembered, suddenly, Corinne telling me there would be 'plenty of time for boys' when I was older. Well, I was eighteen in a couple of months and there still wasn't time for boys.

We had dinner at a restaurant owned by Mr Devine. It reminded me strongly of the hotel restaurant in Milan: the same colour scheme of cream and gold; even the table linen was virtually identical. How long ago that seemed now. The opulence of the room, and the perfect service, didn't intimidate me this time. I knew how to behave.

We had just finished our desserts, when the headwaiter came over with a message for Bella's mother: Mr Devine had phoned to say he would be joining us for coffee.

'Don't be alarmed, Sophie, if Daddy directs all his conversation towards you,' said Bella. 'He says I don't let my friends get a word in edgeways. He is determined to silence me and bring you out of yourself.' I expected Sophie to take this news badly. But she looked perfectly calm.

'I'm sorry – I should have said earlier – but I can't stay for coffee. I'm meeting someone.'

'Who?' I said, more sharply than I meant to. Mrs Devine glanced at me.

'No one you know,' said Sophie. I think it was the only time she ever directly lied to me.

'Oh Sophie, you are a dark horse!' said Bella, 'Is it that boy at the show – you know, the stylist with the nose-ring? I told you he wasn't gay.' Sophie blushed and smiled, pushed her chair back, and got to her feet. 'It is, isn't it!' howled Bella. She seemed to have forgotten all about the 'creepy old guy' at the show. 'Oh well, I want to hear all about it, in the morning.'

'Really, Bella,' said Mrs Devine. She looked at Sophie; I realised she had been looking at her a lot, all evening, though they had hardly spoken.

Sophie thanked Mrs Devine for dinner, and left. It couldn't think of any way to try and stop her without making a scene, so I didn't try: I let her go. Bella's mother watched Sophie until she had disappeared from sight, and then turned to me.

'So tell me, Jen – if it isn't breaking a confidence – is Bella right? Is Sophie meeting a boy?'

'Not a boy, exactly.'

'A man? Older than her?' I sighed and glanced around

the restaurant. I knew Sophie would be furious if I told tales behind her back.

'I don't know who she is meeting. I think he might be older than her − a little bit older, in his twenties. It's just that Sophie seems so young, sometimes. I worry about her. It's silly.'

'No, it isn't silly. It means you are a good friend, you want to protect her.' I squirmed in my seat. I had just lied for Sophie, but somehow I didn't feel like a good friend. There was a long, slightly awkward pause. Mrs Devine set her coffee cup down; it hit the saucer with a loud metallic clink.

'What is it, Mummy?' asked Bella.

'Oh, I was just thinking of a friend of mine − Clarissa. She looked a lot like Sophie. We were models together in Paris, a long time ago. Clarissa got involved with a friend of Giovanni's . . .' she hesitated, and I thought she was going to clam up, or change the subject, '. . . he was a terrible man.'

'What happened?' I said. 'Did he cheat on her? Did they break up?'

'Yes, he cheated on her but they didn't break up. She died. She was seventeen.' It was as if the volume had been turned down on the restaurant. The only voice I could hear was Mrs Devine's. 'Clarissa was so good she couldn't see the evil in other people. She never believed the stories about him and his other girls. He had a string of them, all over town, but he kept them apart − and made them all feel special. He was always phoning Clarissa and sending her little notes and letters when he couldn't see her. She had a drawer full of letters.

'Clarissa blamed his drug use – which was huge, even for the times – on his friends. She said he was misunderstood – no one knew how kind he could be. "He makes me feel desirable," that's what she said to me the day before she died.'

'What happened to her?' asked Bella.

'A drugs overdose. That was the official verdict. But Clarissa never took drugs, she hardly even drank. She was a little old-fashioned. He liked that in his girls. He liked to find a young model who was unspoiled and then – ruin her.

'Before Clarissa there was a fifteen-year-old, a Danish girl, who was besotted with him. I heard rumours that he had passed her around all his friends. She tried to kill herself.

'There was a party at his friend's apartment in Paris – he had boltholes all over Europe – and Clarissa asked me to go but I was working and, besides, I didn't like to be in the same room with him. I detested him. So she went on her own and the next day she was found dead in the bathroom. They had to break the door down. She had locked herself in.

'Giovanni's friend was questioned but there was no case against him. He went to New York for a while and lay low. When he came back to Europe, he was much more discreet in his drugs use and everyone said he was reformed. The scandal was soon forgotten. Clarissa was forgotten. I got out of modelling and went home, to London, where I met your father, Bella. And life went on.'

She just took a sip of mineral water and set the glass down on the table, her hand a little unsteady.

'What are you three looking so serious about?' asked Mr Devine. I hadn't even noticed him arrive at the table.

'Nothing,' said his wife, 'just chitchat about the show today.'

Mr Devine bent down and kissed her on the cheek. 'You're a little pale, Caroline,' he said, 'are you feeling unwell?'

'I'm fine, perfectly fine.'

'Good. Well in that case can I drag you away from the girls, only there's someone I want you to meet . . .'

Mrs Devine almost jumped to her feet. It was as if she had to escape from what she had just said. She was walking away from the table when I stood up and called after her.

'Mrs Devine!'

'Yes?'

'What was the name of the man you mentioned – the friend of Giovanni's?'

'Why do you want to know?' Her voice was calm, almost cold.

'Oh, in case I ever run into him. I'd like to avoid him.'

'Come along, Caroline,' said Mr Devine impatiently, 'you can talk to the girls later.'

'In a minute, Charles. Giovanni's friend? Guido. His name was Guido.' And she turned and walked away.

I sat down again.

'What on earth . . .?' said Bella.

'The man at Giovanni's show – the old guy with Sophie – his name is Guido – I think she's with him now.' I was finding it hard to breathe. Almost before I had got the words out, Bella was on her mobile, texting Sophie.

I took my phone out of my bag. There was a voicemail from Sophie.

Hi, Jen – listen, I'm with Guido at his place. He's having a party – and I wish you were here! You'll like him, really, you just need to get to know him. His friends are here but I'm the only girl . . . so if you get this message just come straight over. Don't be pissed off with me, please, Jen. Right, see you later, bye . . . Oh! I forgot. The address is . . .

Her voice was a little slurred. I handed the phone to Bella. I felt sick.

'Come on,' she said, 'we can be there in ten minutes.'

In the taxi on the way to Guido's I started to worry that this was a big mistake. There was no proof that Guido had done anything to Clarissa, Mrs Devine had admitted as much. I knew Bella was going to barge into the party and drag Sophie out. It would be horribly embarrassing and Sophie would never forgive me. I was going to lose another friend. We were nearly there. I had to say something before it was too late.

'Maybe, I should go in on my own,' I said, nervously.

'She's not expecting us both to turn up. You're not even supposed to know about Guido. I'll tell her everything your mum said – I'll make sure she leaves with me. You don't have to get involved.'

'Don't be stupid. Anything could be going on in there, you can't go in on your own. We have to stick together. And I am involved – if I hadn't taken her to Giovanni's stupid party she would never have met the creep . . . Look! We're here.'

She paid the driver and we got out. Bella was tense – almost excited. I wondered if she was enjoying the drama. 'That must be Guido's place,' she said, pointing to an expensive-looking apartment building. She started to walk.

'Wait,' I said, 'please . . .' I stepped in front of her. 'Go back to the car,' I pleaded. When she cried, 'No!' and pushed me out of the way, I thought, for a second, that she was angry with me.

Then I turned and saw Sophie falling, falling through the air.

22

'She's dead. She's dead.'

There was no blood, I remember thinking that there should have been blood. The girl on the pavement looked as unreal as a broken doll. Her legs were at an odd angle, as though they had been pulled out of position by a naughty child. I didn't scream. I stood, frozen, looking down at Bella crouched next to the body.

'No, Jen, I think she's alive – I think she's breathing!' Bella looked up at me, her face as white as Sophie's and wild with panic. 'Hold her hand – talk to her – I can't – hold her hand!' I knelt on the pavement and Bella staggered to her feet. I took Sophie's hand – it was still warm. The relief of that moment! I felt myself come back to life – just as Bella, who had been so strong, started to break down. She was wailing, 'Oh God, oh God, oh God . . .'

'Bella – shut up! There's no time for that – phone for an ambulance! And the police! Hurry up – do it now!' The wailing stopped. Bella grabbed her phone out of her bag, and dialled.

'You're going to be all right, Sophie,' I told her, holding

her hand tight, 'you're going to be all right. Just hold on, hold on . . .'

'They're on their way,' said Bella, sounding calmer. She kneeled down next to me on the pavement. A few seconds passed, and the street was so silent it was as if nothing had happened, as though no one had noticed. Then the sound of a door opening, footsteps, male voices . . .

We looked up: six or seven men were staring, horrified, at Sophie. And in the middle of the crowd was Guido.

'What have you done to her?' I cried. 'You bastard! You bastard!'

'She jumped . . . I didn't touch her, I swear . . .' said Guido, his voice small and pleading. He reeled back for a moment and then took off down the street. I heard a car door slam and a screech of tyres. Guido's friends started to move off in different directions.

Then – at last – there was a wail of sirens and the police and the paramedics were there, and Sophie was being lifted off the pavement and I let go of her hand.

For two days it was touch and go. Bella and I slept on chairs outside Sophie's room. Mrs Devine was with us most of the time. I don't think she slept at all. Every time I opened my eyes she was sitting up and staring at the closed door of Sophie's private room, as though she could will her to stay alive. We weren't allowed to see her because of the risk of infection; and, besides, we weren't family.

Mr Devine tried to persuade us to come back to the hotel

but his wife just shook her head, and eventually I snapped, 'Just leave us alone, can't you? *Leave us alone.*'

'When Sophie wakes up, Daddy, when we know she's all right, we'll rest then,' said Bella.

Bella and I were interviewed, separately, by the police. Mrs Devine demanded an interview as well, although she was not a witness. She said she had important background information.

The police asked me to recall the smallest, most unimportant details, but they didn't seem interested in what I knew to be true. 'What does it matter what time we arrived at the scene?' I shouted. 'He hurt her. I know Guido's to blame. Why haven't you arrested him?' And the police officer, his expression unreadable, wrote something down in his notebook.

When I asked Mrs Devine how her interview had gone, she said, 'The same – the same as before,' and it was a few minutes before she could speak again. I knew she was thinking of Clarissa. *Guido was questioned but there was no case against him.* The three of us were sitting together, in our usual spot, outside Sophie's room. I heard her take a deep breath, then release it slowly. 'He has got away with it, again, I know. If Sophie lives, I can bear it.' Bella put her arm around her mother.

On the third day the swelling on Sophie's brain went down and the doctors said she was in the clear. Her legs were broken but they would heal. Sophie's parents arrived just in time to hear the good news. They had been on holiday in Spain and had been difficult to trace. Mr Lamb came over to us and managed a couple of sentences of hurried thanks before following his wife into Sophie's room. When they came out Mrs Lamb was crying. They walked past us without a word. I heard Mrs Lamb say to her husband, 'What if she's left with a limp? Did you ever hear of a model with a limp? She'll be finished.' And he said, 'She's alive, Jo, for God's sake, that's all that matters.'

I expected Mrs Devine to wait at the hospital until we were allowed in to see Sophie. But as soon as Mr and Mrs Lamb had left, she got up to go.

'Sophie will want to see her friends – you and Bella. I'm not needed here.' She put her jacket on and straightened her skirt. I reached up and grabbed her hand.

'Thank you,' I said, 'thank you for telling us about Guido.' She smiled but didn't speak.

'Are you going back to the hotel, Mummy?' asked Bella.

Mrs Devine shook her head. 'I'm going to visit Clarissa.' I dropped her hand. 'Oh don't look so startled, the pair of you. I haven't lost my mind. Clarissa is buried in Paris. I didn't go to her funeral. Guido went, for appearances' sake. To stand and look at him while she was laid in the ground . . . it was impossible. I think it is time I said goodbye.'

It was nearly a week before we were allowed to see Sophie. The nurse said only one visitor at a time so I had to go in on my own. I was afraid of how she would look, but it wasn't a doll I saw in the hospital bed, it was Sophie.

'Sorry to have given you such a fright.'

'Don't be daft.'

'Thanks for being there. For, you know, saving my life.'

'Oh, I didn't do anything. Bella was great.'

What happened, Sophie, I wanted to ask, what did he do to you? But the nurses had warned me: no questions, don't upset her, she has to rest. It was Sophie who brought it up.

'You were right about Guido. Not such a nice man, after all.' My stomach lurched.

'Oh God, Sophie – you don't have to talk about him.'

'No, it's OK. I've already told the police. I want to tell you.'

I squeezed her hand. 'Go on – you can tell me anything you like.'

'I was in a club with Guido and he was buying me drinks and I didn't want to look like a little kid so I drank them. And then some of his friends arrived and Guido said we should all go back to his. I didn't like his friends much – they seemed so much older than Guido. And I didn't like the way they looked at me. But I went and for a while it was OK. Someone put some music on and Guido danced with me. It was fun.

'I went to the bathroom and phoned you. I wanted you to see that Guido was OK, and I didn't want to be the only girl at the party. When I came out of the bathroom the music had stopped and, I don't know, everything was different.

One of Guido's friends – he was English, I think his name was Nick – kept asking me to sit on his knee. And when I said no they all laughed.

'And then one of them kissed me and I pushed him away and Guido got angry and said I should be nice to his friends. He said I was going to be nice to all his friends. I got scared and ran out on to the balcony. And I didn't stop running, I just kept running.'

I said how brave she had been, sticking up for herself, and what a sick bastard Guido was. And, over and over again, how glad I was she was OK. I didn't tell her about Clarissa. I didn't know if I would ever tell her. Sophie didn't say anything else about Guido. Not because she couldn't bear to but because she had something else – something better – on her mind.

'I've made a decision, Jen,' and she smiled at me. It wasn't a 'being brave' smile – it was real.

'Yeah?' I said, grinning back at her. 'What's that then?'

'I'm getting out of modelling. I'm going to do something I'm good at, something I'll actually enjoy. I think I'd like to be a teacher. They teach languages in primary schools, you know. I was looking into it, before . . . all this. I'd enjoy working with young kids.' Smart, capable Sophie a languages teacher: yes, that would work.

'You'll be brilliant, Sophie, absolutely brilliant.'

I heard the door open and I turned round, expecting it to be a nurse, coming to tell me my time was up. But it was Bella.

'Is there room for another?' She came over to the bed and pulled up a chair.

'Budge over, Jen, give me some space. I must say, Soph, you don't look nearly as bad as I thought you would. I was expecting a corpse-like pallor.'

'Oh God, Bella!' I stuck my elbow into her ribs.

'What? What have I said? I don't do sensitive, you know that.'

Sophie laughed.

'I can't stay long, I'm not supposed to be here. Honestly, that nurse is so strict. I snuck in when her back was turned – I knew you wouldn't mind, Sophie. So when are you out of here? I expect you'll be off work for a while.'

'Actually, I'm never going back to work.'

Bella looked glum. 'Oh God, Sophie, is it as bad as that? I had no idea.'

'No – I mean, I'll be fine. But I'm not going to model again. I'm going to go back to college and finish my exams. I'm going to be a teacher.'

'Good for you!' squealed Bella. 'Actually, I have a bit of an announcement to make as well: I'm retiring. Well, modelling was never for me, was it? I'm going to talk Hugo's father into giving me a job on the farm – you know, train me up. Mummy tried to hide how relieved she was with some crack about being surprised I didn't want to be a mechanic. But I told her – "Cars are my hobby. Farming is my life." '

She looked almost comically serious, as though she had just announced her intention to devote herself to the poor.

Sophie said she thought Bella would look lovely in Wellington boots and I said maybe the pigs wouldn't mind her bad habits. 'Very intelligent beasts, pigs,' said Bella, 'and they'll be organic pigs, don't forget that.'

And then Sophie said, 'That just leaves you, Jen. Out of the three of us – you're the only one who is still a model.'

And I realised, with a jolt, that she was right. I was completely on my own.

23

I got up this morning, at 5.30 a.m., showered, ate a breakfast of tropical fruits and yoghurt and then went out on to the veranda and took in the view for one last time.

It's a good view, don't get me wrong. The sand is white and the sea and sky are almost too blue to be true. It's perfect. Celebrities pay thousands of pounds a night for this view. I hate it. It's flat and lifeless, like the work of a second-rate photographer. It is too beautiful.

There is no one here I can say this to, no one who would understand my hatred of the view.

It was my eighteenth birthday last night and I celebrated it with people I hardly know, people who only invited me here because they want to be seen with me. The host is a businessman who likes to surround himself with beautiful and creative young people. If it is reported that I am staying on the island as his guest it will make him look good. Susy and Jack from the *Clothes Crease* crowd are also along for the ride but they are staying in cheaper accommodation because they are not as important as I am.

Susy is exactly as she was the last time I saw her – she

even did her crazy dance, last night on the beach – but Jack has changed. The failure of his magazine has changed him. Last night he made several barbed comments about my 'mainstream success'. He gave me a wrap of coke to hide his hostility to me, to pretend to himself that he does not mind my wealth, my success. He slipped the wrap into my pocket and said, 'Happy birthday,' and Susy smiled and clapped her hands. Sophie is recuperating with her family, Bella is on holiday with Hugo, and Stevie is lost to me. I am here because I did not want to be alone on my eighteenth birthday.

Jack's present disgusted me. I stumbled away and found a place on the beach, away from the crowd. I meant to throw the coke in the sea or bury it in the sand but I took it – my first and last line of coke – because I was so unhappy I could not think what else to do. Only I wasn't alone. A photographer saw me, caught me. And I knew that when she sold the photos the press would gather like wolves around me, and this time they would not hold back, they would not draw in their claws.

There is an unwritten rule of celebrity life: you can survive one or two scandals in quick succession but not three – three strikes and you're out. At least until you stage your comeback. My mother the thief was number one; being at the scene of another model's attempted suicide – that's what the press called it – was number two; exposed as a drug addict would have been number three.

Elegance would not have stood for it. They hired me for

my freshness and purity and I am becoming associated with sleaze. I am spoiling the picture. It is almost funny: I have been drunk once in my life; I have taken drugs once. It's not much for an eighteen-year-old, is it? My true failures – the things that make me ashamed – the press know and care nothing about.

I couldn't bear to be torn apart in public for the wrong reasons. So I begged and pleaded with the photographer. And a miracle happened: she destroyed the pictures. Maybe because she is young and a girl, like me, she took pity. She gave me a second chance. I'm going to take it. I'm flying out of here this morning and I am never, ever, coming back.

Epilogue

Corinne took the news badly. She just couldn't help herself.

'Walk away from your career now and you'll be finished – forgotten. The business has a short memory. By the time you try to come back, younger girls will have taken your place. You'll be a nobody again. Is that what you want?'

'I'll take the risk.'

She slumped back in her chair, defeated, and looked at me with real dislike. I could see her point: nothing so hateful as an ungrateful protégée.

'Well, Elegance are cooling on you anyway. After that Sophie business . . . they won't be sorry to see the back of you. I've been trying to persuade them not to use the release clause in the contract. Now I won't have to bother. I suppose you'll do the press interviews we have scheduled for you this week. Or will I have to cancel those as well?'

'Of course I'll do the interviews.'

She picked up her phone: 'Madeleine – could you send up the next girl please?'

When she put the phone down, I said, 'Another new face?'

'There's always a new face,' snapped Corinne. 'Now if you don't mind, I have an appointment.'

I got up, walked to the door and opened it. Then I thought: no, she doesn't get to have the last word. I slammed the door shut, turned round and walked back – and sat down again in the big purple chair, for one last time.

'You know, Corinne, there's a whole world out there and you're missing it.'

'I don't know . . .' She was wide-eyed with surprise.

'You don't know what I mean, do you? All that matters to you is the business. Well that's fine – for you. But it's not all that matters to me. I want a life – I want to see my friends and my family, and I want to take risks – maybe have my heart broken a few times. I want all the things that make life messy – all the things that get in the way of work. And the next girl who walks into this office – the girl who is on her way up now – I bet she wants all those things too. *She will want to have a life!* Let her have it, Corinne. Because if you stop her, it doesn't make you a great agent – it makes you a lousy human being.'

There was a knock on the door. Corinne didn't move; she was staring at me, speechless. I got up and let the new girl in. And then I walked away.

I bumped into Madja in reception. She was wearing a zebra striped coat and the hat with the eyes.

'Jen, dearie, how are you? And how is poor Sophie?'

'I'm fine – and Sophie's on the mend. She said to thank you for the flowers.'

Madja leaned in close and whispered, 'You know I spoke to Bella's mother and she told me all about Guido. I can't say I was surprised – I remember the rumours about him back in the eighties. Well, I've put the word out: he'll find a lot of doors closed to him from now on. Even Giovanni has been persuaded to drop his old pal.' I threw my arms around her and thanked her. After the scene with Corinne I was feeling a bit emotional.

I could see over Madja's shoulder, on the wall behind Madeleine's desk, five of my best photos from the Elegance campaign. I had replaced Francine Hope on the wall. I wondered who would replace me. I had a pang of regret. Madja patted my back and gently disentangled herself.

'Madja, I've resigned from the agency, I'm giving up modelling – I've just told Corinne. It's time I did something else.'

'I don't suppose I can persuade you to change your mind?' I shook my head. 'No, I didn't think so. You're a smart girl. You'll do well, whatever you do. And you know, you can always try and come back. You're an exceptional model – you won't be easy to replace.'

'Really?'

'Well ... don't stay away too long. Everybody gets forgotten in the end. And, Jen, don't leave at all unless you are absolutely sure.'

'It's all right,' and suddenly it was. 'I'm sure. I'm absolutely sure.'

* * *

My last media interview. And it's for a tiny digital channel, GTV.

The GTV people can't believe their luck. A routine interview has become an event. They show a montage of my greatest hits – shots of me on the runway in London, Paris, Milan and New York; stills from my biggest advertising campaigns; there is even footage I didn't know existed, of me off-duty, arriving at parties.

One clip brings tears to my eyes: me, Bella and Sophie, playing the English family, on the runway together in Milan. Lucy Hayling was right: I look beautiful. I can see it at last. And the music playing as we walk awkwardly down the runway is the Arctic Monkeys' 'Fluorescent Adolescent' – the last track on Stevie's 'Songs for Jennifer'. I played that song so much when I was alone in hotel rooms, or travelling between jobs. And when I was too tired to think, the ache of longing in the song made me feel what I had lost.

The interviewer asks me what my plans are.

'I'm not sure yet. I might go to college and study to be a fashion designer. Or I might take a year off. What I really want to do is spend more time with my friends. I've lost touch with some old friends and I really regret it. I regret it so much.' And I look straight into the camera.

When the interview is over, I check with the director that they have everything they need. He gushes his thanks. Then he calls over a runner and tells him to show me to my car. He calls the runner 'you'. I've been on enough TV sets to know why: a runner is the lowest of the low, an absolute beginner.

The runner walks me to my car. I like the look of him – he's not trying too hard to be cool. He could be the boy next door. He is so clearly star-struck in my presence it's weird – and kind of sweet. I can see him struggling to think of something to say. I decide to help him out.

'What's your name?'

'D-Dan.' He can hardly say his own name he is so nervous. And then he smiles. I'm surprised at the self-assurance, the confidence, in that smile. 'I have difficulty saying my name when I meet models.'

'How many models do you know?'

'Only one – Lucy Hayling. I think you know her?' Lucy, lovely Lucy, who told me I was beautiful in a man's suit and stopped me throwing my career away in Milan. So that now, today, I can end it on my own terms.

I'm so pleased to have met a friend of Lucy's, today of all days, that when we reach the car, I don't get in. I stand and chat with Dan. And he really opens up.

'. . . Yeah, so I dropped out of college – I've come to London to seek my fortune.' He actually uses those words: *seek my fortune.* He reminds me of myself, two years ago: ambitious, eager to please. And desperate to leave his old life behind. He has no idea what the cost might be.

Dan is about my age, maybe a little younger, but I feel so much older. I feel like his mother.

'Here, Dan – take my card. If you ever feel the need

to get in touch, just drop me an email, or phone me.'

He looks amazed, delighted.

'God – really? Thanks – thanks!'

Oh no. Maybe he thinks I'm inviting him to make a pass – maybe he thinks I'm coming on to him. But no, it's all right, panic over. He is gazing at my card with a big dopey grin on his face – like a kid who has just got his favourite football player's autograph. I'm sure he hasn't got the wrong idea. All the same, I feel concerned for him. Maybe because he is a friend of Lucy's and I owe her. Maybe because he's another small-town kid, trying to make it big.

'Don't let the industry get you down,' I say. He looks puzzled, so I try again. 'Everyone will want to push you around, make a killing out of your talent. But you've got to make your career work for you. Grab the best of it and run. Put yourself first.' I hug him, give him a quick peck on the cheek, and get in the back of the car.

As the car pulls away I see him walking away, head up, shoulders back. He is almost swaggering. I feel a little uneasy. Suddenly I know what I should have said to him: be true to yourself and remember who your real friends are. Nothing more complicated than that. Well it's too late now and I guess it doesn't matter. He'll have forgotten his encounter with Jennifer Jones, ex-supermodel, in a day or two.

I take my phone out of my bag. I have to do this now.

'Hello?' A girl's voice. I almost hang up. Then I ask if Stevie is there.

'Is that Jen? Jen, it's Clare. Stevie's upstairs. He's staying

219

with us, until his mum gets their new place sorted out. I'll get him for you.' Suddenly I'm very afraid: afraid of what he'll say; afraid he'll refuse to come to the phone.

'Clare, no – wait. I just want to say, in case he doesn't want to speak to me, how sorry I am, for reacting the way I did when I found out you two were together. And I want to say sorry to you too. I'm just so sorry about everything.'

'It's OK, Jen. I think we should have told you earlier. It must have been a shock, finding out that way. It's OK. And though I shouldn't speak for Stevie, I have a feeling he'll be glad you've called. You know, he was watching you, just now, on TV.'

'Was he?' The relief is so strong, I almost laugh. It must mean something, mustn't it? He can bear to look at me on TV.

'Hang on, Jen. Don't go away – I'll get him for you.' I hear her calling his name. There's a long pause, then muffled voices: *It's Jen – she says she's really sorry, for everything, just talk to her . . . you know you want to . . .*

'Hello, Jen.' It's Stevie. He's speaking to me. I think: I'll apologise in a minute. There's something else I want to say.

'Hello, Stevie. I was just wondering if you and Clare are free at the weekend. Only I'd like you to meet some friends of mine – Sophie and Bella. Bella is having a birthday party – it's her eighteenth – and I'd love you both to come. So can you come? Please say you'll come.'